SWEET LOST AND FOUND

A SWEET COVE MYSTERY
BOOK 26

J. A. WHITING

Formatting by Signifer Book Design

Proofreading by Donna Rich: donnarich@me.com and Riann Kohrs

To hear about new books and book sales, please sign up for my mailing list at:
jawhiting.com

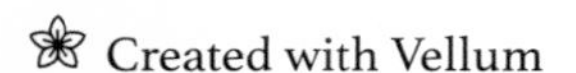

With thanks to my readers

Use your magic for good

1

The warm spring breeze danced through the streets of Sweet Cove, Massachusetts, carrying the scent of blooming flowers and the salty tang of the nearby ocean. The quaint seaside town was bustling with activity as locals and tourists enjoyed the warm, sunny weather while strolling along the brick side-walks and browsing the charming shops that lined Main Street.

Around the corner from Main Street at the Victorian mansion that housed some of the Rose-land sisters' various businesses, the day had been filled with its usual hustle and bustle.

Angie, with her honey-blonde hair pulled back in a ponytail, had spent most of the day in her Sweet Dreams Bake Shop, her baking filling the air with the irresistible aroma of fresh pastries. Her twin sister Jenna, with her long brown hair braided neatly down her back, had been hard at work in her jewelry shop crafting delicate pieces that sparkled in the sunlight. Courtney, the youngest sister, with her bright smile and quick wit, had spent the day at the art gallery with Mr. Finch, discussing upcoming exhibitions and rearranging displays, and Ellie, the tall, graceful middle sister, had been busy running the bed-and-breakfast, ensuring their guests had a comfortable and memorable stay.

As the late afternoon sun cast a golden glow over the town, the four sisters and Mr. Finch, their "adopted" family member, gathered on the expansive front porch of their home, enjoying a well-deserved break. They sat in comfortable wicker chairs, enjoying the warm breeze and watching as Euclid, a large orange Maine Coon, and Circe, a sleek black cat, lazed contentedly on the porch railing.

Angie leaned back in her chair, stretching her arms above her head. "What a day. I swear, the whole town must have a sweet tooth today. I could barely keep up with the orders."

Jenna chuckled. "I'm sure they just couldn't resist the smell of your famous cherry pie."

Courtney nodded in agreement, her blue eyes twinkling. "I actually had a couple come into the gallery asking if we sold your pies there," she told her older sister. "I almost sent them on a wild goose chase just for fun."

"Courtney," Ellie admonished, but her expression was full of amusement. "You wouldn't really do that, would you?"

"Of course not." Courtney grinned. "I sent them straight to Angie's bakery. I couldn't let them miss out on that pie."

The sisters laughed, the sound mingling with the chirping of birds and the distant crash of waves against the shore, but as their laughter faded, a strange silence fell over the porch. Angie and Courtney exchanged a look, their smiles fading slightly.

"Do you feel it?" Angie asked, her voice low.

Courtney nodded slowly. "Something feels ... off. I can't quite put my finger on it, but there's this weird unease settling over me."

"I've felt it all day as well," Mr. Finch told them.

Jenna and Ellie looked at their sisters and Mr. Finch with concern. They knew better than to dismiss the intuitive powers that ran in their family.

"What kind of feeling is it?" Jenna asked, leaning forward in her chair.

Angie's eyes narrowed while she thought about it, trying to pin down the sensation. "It's like... a shadow passing over the sun. Everything looks bright, but there's this darkness under it all."

Courtney added, "It's like the calm before a storm. Something's coming, but I don't know what."

Ellie suddenly sat up straight, her blue eyes widening. "Chief Martin is on his way," she announced matter-of-factly. "He'll tell us what's going on."

The other sisters turned to look at her, knowing Ellie's uncanny ability to sense the chief's approach. They didn't question it; they simply waited, their eyes scanning the quiet street.

Sure enough, within minutes, a police cruiser turned onto their street and pulled into the driveway. Chief Phillip Martin, a stocky man in his mid-fifties with graying hair at his temples, stepped out of the car. His face was set in a serious expression as he approached the porch.

Courtney sighed. "Uh oh. I can tell by the look on his face that trouble has landed."

The chief climbed the porch steps, his shoes making a soft thud against the wooden boards.

"Afternoon," he greeted them, his voice warm despite the tension in his shoulders. "It's a beautiful day."

Euclid and Circe perked up at the chief's arrival, jumping down from their perch to weave between his legs. Chief Martin chuckled, bending down to scratch behind their ears and under their chins. The cats purred loudly, momentarily lightening the mood.

Ellie stood up, smoothing down her sundress. "I'll go make some coffee," she said, disappearing into the house.

Mr. Finch, who had been quietly observing from his rocking chair, leaned forward. "How are things, Phillip?" he asked, his voice laced with concern.

The chief sighed, straightening up and looking at their faces. "I may as well just tell you. You can probably sense why I'm here."

Angie nodded, her eyes serious. "We've felt something off all day. Why don't you wait for Ellie to come back with the coffee?" she suggested.

Chief Martin agreed, settling into an empty chair. The group fell into an uneasy silence, broken only by the gentle creaking of Mr. Finch's rocking chair and the soft purring of the cats.

The chief had known the Roseland sisters since

they were little kids. Their grandmother had lived in Sweet Cove in a cottage on Robin's Point down near Coveside, and she'd had strong paranormal powers she'd used to assist the chief on some cases. Her family had spent many happy summers with her in her little house by the sea.

Growing up, the sisters never knew that their mother and grandmother had "special skills." It was only after moving to Sweet Cove that the four Rose-lands had discovered they were descended from women with supernatural powers, and as they settled in, their own skills began to emerge.

A few minutes later, Ellie returned, balancing a tray with steaming mugs of coffee, a small pitcher of cream, and a sugar bowl. She set it down on the wicker table in the center of their circle, and everyone helped themselves.

Once they were all settled with their drinks, Chief Martin took a deep breath. "Lincoln Harrington and his wife Rose Putnam Harrington live in Silver Cove," he began.

Courtney's eyes lit up with recognition. "We've heard of them," she said. "They're generous benefac-tors for lots of cultural institutions in the area."

The chief nodded. "Correct. They are also art

collectors. Last night they were robbed of several very valuable paintings by master artists."

A collective gasp went up from the group. Mr. Finch's face creased with worry. "Oh, no," he said, his voice trembling slightly. "Are the Harringtons all right?"

Chief Martin held up a hand to reassure them. "Mrs. Harrington was in the hospital for surgery, and Mr. Harrington was sound asleep in his bed. He didn't stir during the robbery even though at one point the thieves were in his bedroom." He paused, taking a sip of his coffee. "The man is known for being a very deep sleeper. He also has a hearing impairment and uses a hearing aid."

Euclid, who had been lounging at the chief's feet, let out a low hiss, as if sensing the seriousness of the situation.

Courtney's eyes darkened. "What paintings were stolen?" she asked.

The chief's expression grew dark. "A Renoir, two Dürers, a Pissaro, and a Monet."

"Good grief," Mr. Finch exclaimed, clearly flabbergasted. His bushy eyebrows shot up nearly to his hairline.

"The thieves knew what they were after," the

chief continued. "They left behind other paintings that were less valuable."

Circe, picking up on the tension, began swishing her tail back and forth in agitation.

Jenna, who had been quietly listening, spoke up. "Any security footage?" she asked, her voice calm but her eyes sharp.

"Some," Chief Martin replied, taking another sip of his coffee. "I'd like all of you to come to the crime scene this evening if you can."

The sisters exchanged glances, a silent conversation passing between them. They all nodded in agreement.

"We'll be there," Angie said firmly. "What time would you like us to meet you?"

"Let's say 7 PM," the chief suggested. "That should give us enough time to gather all the preliminary information."

With the plan set, Chief Martin finished his coffee and stood to leave. The sisters and Mr. Finch walked him to his car, thanking him for coming to inform them personally.

As the police cruiser pulled out of the driveway and disappeared down the street, the Roseland sisters and Mr. Finch returned to the porch. The peaceful atmosphere from earlier had vanished, replaced by anticipation and worry.

“Well,” Courtney said. “I guess that explains the weird feeling we've had all day.”

Angie nodded, absentmindedly running her fingers through her hair. “I just can't believe someone would break into a private home and steal such valuable paintings. The nerve of it.”

“And to think they were in the same room as Mr. Harrington while he slept,” Jenna added, shaking her head in disbelief. “It must have been terrifying for him when he woke up and realized what had happened.”

Ellie, who had been quiet since the chief's departure, spoke up. “I wonder why they chose now to strike. With Mrs. Harrington in the hospital, it seems like they were waiting for an opportunity.”

Mr. Finch nodded sagely. “Indeed, Miss Ellie. It does seem like this was a carefully planned operation. These thieves must have been watching the Harringtons for some time.”

“But how did they know Mrs. Harrington was in the hospital?” Courtney wondered aloud. “And how did they know they could snoop around the Harringtons’ bedroom without Mr. Harrington hearing them?”

“Those are excellent questions, Miss Courtney,” Mr. Finch said, his eyes shining with the excitement of a new mystery. “I'm sure we'll find out more when we visit the crime scene this evening.”

Angie stood up. “Well, I don't know about you, but I think I need to bake something. It always helps me think.”

Jenna laughed. “Only you would respond to a crime by baking, Angie.”

“Hey, it works,” Angie protested with a grin. “Besides, we might need some snacks for our investigation later. Who knows how long we'll be at the Harringtons' house?”

The sisters all agreed that some baked goods wouldn't go wrong, and they trooped into the kitchen to help Angie. As they worked, mixing batter and rolling out dough, they continued to speculate about the robbery.

“I wonder if the paintings have already left the country,” Courtney mused as she sifted flour into a bowl.

“It's possible,” Jenna replied, carefully measuring out vanilla extract, “but moving such valuable and recognizable artworks can't be easy. They'd need some serious connections.”

“Maybe they're not planning to sell them,” Ellie

suggested, greasing a baking pan. "Some collectors will pay to have famous artworks stolen just so they can keep them for themselves."

Mr. Finch, who had settled himself at the kitchen table with a cup of tea, nodded in agreement. "That's true, Miss Ellie. The black market for art is surprisingly large and complex."

As the smell of baking cookies began to fill the kitchen, Angie paused in her work, a thoughtful expression on her face. "You know," she said slowly, "I have a feeling this case is going to be more complicated than it seems on the surface."

The others looked at her, knowing better than to dismiss Angie's intuitions.

"What do you mean?" Jenna asked.

Angie shrugged, struggling to put her feeling into words. "I'm not sure exactly. It's just... there's something about this whole situation that doesn't quite add up."

Courtney nodded, her face serious. "I feel it too. There's more to this story than a simple robbery, even if it was a high-stakes one."

Mr. Finch leaned forward. "Well, my dears, it seems we have quite the mystery on our hands. I, for one, am looking forward to seeing what we can uncover at the Harringtons' house this evening."

As the kitchen timer dinged, signaling the first batch of cookies was ready, the Roseland sisters exchanged determined looks. Whatever secrets lay hidden behind the theft of the Harringtons' paintings, they were ready to uncover them.

Euclid and Circe, who had been watching the baking proceedings with great interest from on top of the refrigerator, meowed in unison, as if adding their own determination to solve the case.

Angie laughed and looked up at the fine felines. "Don't worry, you two," she said. "I'm sure you'll play your part in solving this mystery too."

As the afternoon sun began to dip toward the horizon, casting long shadows across the town, the Roseland sisters, Mr. Finch, and their feline companions prepared themselves for the investigation ahead. Little did they know, the theft of the Harringtons' paintings was just the beginning of a case that would test both their skills and their courage.

2

The sun was just beginning to dip below the horizon as Ellie's van wound its way through the picturesque streets of the nearby town of Silver Cove. The four Roseland sisters and Mr. Finch sat in comfortable silence, each lost in their own thoughts about the case that lay ahead.

As they turned onto a dead-end street lined with magnificent homes, Courtney let out a low whistle. "Would you look at these places?" she marveled, her blue eyes wide as she took in the sprawling estates. "I knew this part of Silver Cove was fancy, but this street is something else."

Angie nodded in agreement, her hair catching the last rays of sunlight. "It's like stepping into another world," she murmured.

At the very end of the street, standing proudly on the right, was a stately mansion that seemed to dwarf even its impressive neighbors. The Harrington estate occupied one of the town's choicest private lots, its twenty acres of manicured grounds sloping gently down a slight hill to offer a breathtaking view of the ocean beyond.

Ellie guided the van up the long, winding driveway, lined on both sides by perfectly trimmed hedges and elegant statuary. As they approached the house, its grandeur became even more apparent. The mansion was a masterpiece of classic New England architecture, with gleaming white clapboard siding, black shutters, and a series of gabled roofs that gave it a regal, almost castle-like appearance.

“My word,” Mr. Finch breathed, leaning forward in his seat to get a better look. “It's absolutely magnificent.”

Jenna, always the practical one, furrowed her brow. “It must take an army to maintain a place like this.”

As they drew closer, they could see expansive gardens stretching out behind the house, a riot of spring color even in the fading light. To one side, partially hidden by a stand of old-growth trees, was what appeared to be a private helipad.

Ellie pulled the van to a stop in front of a large carriage house that had been converted into a multi-car garage. As they all climbed out, Courtney hurried around to help Mr. Finch. She offered her arm, which he took gratefully, leaning heavily on his cane with the other hand.

"Thank you, my dear," he said with a warm smile. "These old bones aren't quite as spry as they used to be."

"You're just fine, Mr. Finch." Courtney smiled at the man.

Together, the group made their way up the wide stone steps to the front door, where Chief Martin was waiting for them. His face was drawn and serious, the lines around his eyes deeper than usual.

"Evening, everyone," he greeted them, his voice low. "Thanks for coming out here on such short notice."

Angie stepped forward, her eyes filled with concern. "Of course, Chief. How are the Harringtons holding up?"

The chief sighed, running a hand through his graying hair. "As well as can be expected, I suppose. Mrs. Harrington is still in the hospital. We'll be able to interview her tomorrow." He paused, his expression troubled. "Mr. Harrington is here in the house, but we won't be speaking with him this evening. He's still pretty shaken up by what happened."

Mr. Finch nodded solemnly. "Understandable. It must be quite a shock to wake up and find your home has been invaded and your treasures stolen."

"Indeed," the chief agreed. He gestured for them to follow him inside. "Let me give you a tour and show you how we think the robbery went down."

As they stepped into the grand foyer, with its soaring ceiling and gleaming marble floor, the chief began to explain the situation in more detail. "We're looking at artwork probably worth upwards of forty million dollars," he said, his voice echoing slightly in the cavernous space. "And here's the thing - the thieves seemed to know exactly which paintings to take. Either they got incredibly lucky, or..."

"Or someone told them what to look for," Jenna finished, her eyes narrowing thoughtfully.

The chief nodded grimly. "Exactly."

He led them through the house, starting in a bright sunroom at the back of the property. Large windows offered a panoramic view of the gardens, but one pane was now covered with a sheet of plywood.

"This is where they broke in," the chief explained. "They smashed the window, then reached in to unlock the door."

From there, they moved through a series of opulent rooms - the living room with its plush furnishings, the formal dining room with a table that could easily seat twenty, and the wood-paneled study that smelled of leather and old books. In each room, the chief pointed out bare spots on the walls where paintings had clearly hung until very recently.

"And here," the chief said as they entered the primary bedroom, "is where Mr. Harrington was sleeping through the whole thing."

Courtney shuddered, looking at the enormous four-poster bed. "How terrifying," she murmured, "to think they were in here while he was sleeping..."

After completing their tour of the crime scene, the chief led them back to the kitchen. It was a chef's dream, all gleaming stainless steel and polished granite, but tonight it served a different purpose. The chief gestured to several monitors set up on the large island in the center of the room.

"This is where we've been reviewing the security footage," he explained, pressing a button to start the playback. “It's grainy, but you can see the path they took.”

The sisters and Mr. Finch crowded around, watching intently as two shadowy figures moved across the screens. They saw the thieves make their way through the vast backyard, ignoring the beautiful gardens and the helipad as they headed straight for the sunroom.

“Look at that,” Jenna pointed out. “They're going right for it. They must have known the layout of the house.”

The chief nodded. “That's what we're thinking too.”

As the grainy footage continued, they watched in disbelief as the robbers helped themselves to snacks from the refrigerator and drinks from the liquor cabinet.

“Well, I never!” Mr. Finch exclaimed, his bushy eyebrows shooting up in indignation. “The nerve of them!”

“It gets worse,” the chief warned, fast-forwarding slightly. “Watch this.”

The next scene showed the thieves in the living room, slashing open decorative pillows from the sofa. Stuffing flew everywhere as they shoved priceless paintings into the makeshift sacks.

Ellie gasped. "They didn't even bring proper cases for the artwork? They could have damaged them."

"Looks like they used a bucket for fireplace logs to carry the smaller items they stole," Angie observed, pointing to the screen where a thief was filling an old brass bucket with what appeared to be two small paintings.

The chief stopped the playback, his face grim. "When Mr. Harrington woke up at 7 a.m., he found his glasses and hearing aid on the floor. His wallet was gone from the bedside table, along with one of his watches." He gestured back toward the bedroom. "And of course, those empty spots on the walls are where the paintings used to be."

"How awful," Courtney murmured, her face pale. "He must have been so confused and frightened."

The chief nodded. "There was a trail of footprints leading through the backyard, showing their escape route." He paused, his expression thoughtful. "One thing that's interesting - the Harringtons had their collection appraised for insurance purposes about a year ago. All of the most valuable pieces, the ones with the highest appraisals, were the exact ones that were taken."

Jenna's eyes narrowed. "That seems... convenient. Almost too convenient."

"You're not wrong," the chief agreed. "There have been some whispers, insinuations that the Harringtons might have orchestrated this themselves for the insurance payout."

Mr. Finch looked shocked. "Surely not. From everything I've heard, the Harringtons are pillars of the community."

The chief held up a hand. "I agree, Mr. Finch. It's nonsense, in my opinion. The Harringtons are fabulously wealthy - this insurance payout, as large as it might be, would hardly make a dent in their fortune. There'd be no reason for them to do something like this."

Angie nodded slowly, her intuition tingling. "But someone wanted us to think they might have, didn't they? By taking only the most valuable pieces..."

"Exactly," the chief said, looking impressed. "It's almost like whoever did this wanted to cast suspicion on the Harringtons themselves."

He turned back to the monitors, starting the footage again. "Now, there's one more thing I want to show you. Watch closely."

The sisters and Mr. Finch leaned in, their eyes

glued to the screens. As the thieves made their escape across the backyard, a figure could be seen lurking at the edge of the property.

"Who's that?" Courtney asked, pointing. "They don't seem to be with the robbers."

The chief nodded. "Good eye. This figure doesn't participate in the heist at all. They just... watch."

"A lookout, perhaps?" Mr. Finch suggested.

"Maybe," the chief said. "Or it could be a neighbor who heard something, or was out walking a dog. Or..."

"A rival thief?" Jenna finished the chief's statement, her voice quiet but certain.

The room fell silent as they all contemplated this new piece of the puzzle. The mystery of the Harrington robbery was growing more intriguing by the minute.

Angie was the first to speak. "Chief, do you mind if we take a look around the grounds? Sometimes being in the space can help us pick up on things."

The chief nodded, understanding the sisters' unique abilities. "Of course. Just be careful not to disturb anything. We're still processing the scene."

As they made their way back outside, the last of the daylight had faded, leaving the expansive grounds bathed in the soft glow of the landscape lighting. The sisters and Mr. Finch spread out, each drawn to a different area.

Jenna stood near the broken window of the sunroom, her fingers hovering just above the jagged edge of glass still in the frame. She closed her eyes, concentrating. “There's... fear here,” she murmured. “But also... excitement? It's hard to tell.”

Courtney wandered along the escape route, her eyes scanning the ground. “The footprints are still visible,” she called out. “They were in a hurry, but...” she paused, crouching down to look closer. “It's odd. Some of these prints look different. Could they have changed shoes partway through? Maybe it’s just that some of the prints have dried out.”

Ellie had made her way over to the helipad, her brow furrowed in concentration. “I keep getting flashes,” she said, her voice distant, “of... rotors spinning? But not recently. It's like an echo of something that happened before.”

Angie, meanwhile, had found herself drawn to a particular spot near the edge of the property. She stood still, her eyes closed, breathing deeply. When she opened them, she looked troubled. “This is where that figure was standing,” she said, “the one who was watching.”

Mr. Finch, who had been observing from the patio, walked over and nodded sagely. “It seems, my dears, that we have quite the mystery on our hands. This is no simple robbery - there are layers here to be uncovered.”

As if in agreement, a cool breeze rustled through the trees, carrying with it the salty smell of the nearby ocean. The Roseland sisters looked at one another. Whatever secrets the Harrington estate was hiding, they were ready to uncover them.

The chief joined them on the patio, his face etched with concern. “Well?” he asked. “What do you think? Did you sense anything?”

Angie took a deep breath, looking out over the moonlit grounds. “I think, Chief,” she said slowly, “that we're going to need to dig into this one. This case might not be what it seems on the surface. There might be something we're not seeing yet.”

The others nodded in agreement, each lost in their own thoughts about what they'd seen and felt. As they prepared to leave, promising the chief they'd be in touch with any insights, there was a shared sense of anticipation among them. The Harrington art heist promised to be a puzzle.

As Ellie's van pulled away from the magnificent estate, leaving behind the twinkling lights of Silver

Cove, the Roseland sisters and Mr. Finch knew one thing for certain ... their quiet spring in Sweet Cove was about to become very interesting indeed.

3

In the growing darkness of the evening, the warm glow of lamplight spilled from the windows of the Victorian mansion. Inside, the Roseland sisters, Mr. Finch, and their feline companions had gathered in the cozy family room, each finding their favorite spot as they settled in to discuss the day's events.

Angie curled up in the oversized armchair by the fireplace with Euclid purring contentedly in her lap. As she absently stroked the orange cat's soft fur, her gaze drifted around the room, taking in the familiar details of their beloved home. Sometimes, it still amazed her how they had come to own this magnificent place.

"You know," she said softly, breaking the quiet that had fallen over the group, "I was just thinking about how we ended up here. It still seems like something out of a storybook sometimes."

Jenna, seated cross-legged on the floor with her back against the sofa, looked up from the notebook where she'd been jotting down their observations from the Harrington estate. "You mean how you inherited the house?" she asked, a small smile playing on her lips. "It is pretty incredible when you think about it."

Courtney, sprawled on the sofa with Circe curled up beside her, chuckled. "Remember how shocked we all were when that lawyer showed up at the bakery? I thought Angie was going to faint when she heard the news about the Professor."

Angie laughed, shaking her head at the memory. "Can you blame me? It's not every day you're told you've inherited a mansion from a relative you didn't even know existed."

Mr. Finch, settled comfortably in his favorite rocking chair, leaned forward with interest. "I don't believe I've ever heard the full story," he said. "Would you mind sharing it with an older man?"

Ellie, who had been gazing out the window at the darkened street, turned back to the group. "It's quite a tale," she said, moving to perch on the arm of Angie's chair. "That lawyer who showed up in

Angie's bake shop that day was the man I ended up marrying."

Mr. Finch's bushy eyebrows shot up in surprise. "It was Jack?"

"It sure was." Jenna smiled.

Angie nodded solemnly. "The previous owner of this house was a woman named Professor Marion Linden. She was a town selectman for many years and had retired from teaching mathematics at a university in Boston. She'd lived in Sweet Cove off and on since she was a little girl. Her house, our huge Victorian, was just around the corner from the original Sweet Dreams Bake Shop. The professor and her late husband purchased the house many years ago, and even though Professor Linden admitted that the place was much too large for her, she'd decided that she would never sell it. We had no idea she was related to us until after she died."

"She'd been poisoned," Ellie told Mr. Finch.

"Oh, I remember that. How dreadful," Mr. Finch murmured, shaking his head sadly.

"It was," Angie agreed. "But here's where it gets strange. Professor Linden had no children, no close family that anyone knew of, but she'd done extensive research into her family tree, and somehow she'd discovered that we were very, very distant relatives."

Courtney picked up the thread of the story. "She'd been a daily visitor to Angie's bakery. I guess she felt a connection with her."

"So, when she wrote her will," Ellie explained, "she left most everything to Angie. The house, her savings, even Euclid here." She reached over to scratch the cat behind his ears, earning a contented purr.

"I still can't believe it sometimes," Angie said, looking around at the beautiful room. "This amazing house, a new life in Sweet Cove for all of us ... all because of a distant relative we never even knew we had."

Mr. Finch smiled warmly. "It seems Professor Linden's legacy lives on through all of you. I'd say she chose her heir wisely."

Silence fell over the room as they all reflected on the strange twists of fate that had brought them to this moment. It was Jenna who finally steered the conversation back to the matter at hand.

"Speaking of legacies," she said, flipping back through her notebook, "let's talk about the Harringtons. Specifically, where did Mr. Harrington get his wealth?"

Courtney sat up straighter, dislodging Circe, who gave her an indignant look before resettling. "Oh, I did some digging on that," she said eagerly. "It's actually really impressive. Mr. Harrington started out owning a manufacturing company that produced materials for plumbing and heating systems."

"Not the most glamorous business," Ellie remarked with a slight smile.

"Maybe not," Courtney agreed, "but it was very successful. However, what really increased his fortune was his skill as an investor. Apparently, he has quite a knack for playing the stock market. He's made millions through smart investments alone."

Mr. Finch nodded thoughtfully. "A self-made man, then. That's admirable."

"It is," Angie agreed. "But it also makes me wonder... with all that wealth, why would someone target his art collection? Surely there are easier things to steal that would be worth just as much?"

A knowing look passed over Mr. Finch's face. "As it happens," he said, leaning forward slightly, "I may have some insight into that. I took the liberty of contacting an old friend of mine – Brooks Stonington."

The sisters exchanged curious glances.

"Brooks Stonington?" Jenna repeated. "Why does that name sound familiar?"

"You may have heard of him," Mr. Finch explained. "He's a wealthy amateur sleuth, known for his work in recovering stolen art. I thought his expertise might be valuable in this case."

"That's brilliant, Mr. Finch!" Courtney exclaimed. "What did he have to say?"

Mr. Finch's expression grew serious. "He warned that art thefts are often not as straightforward as they appear. In fact, he shared a rather intriguing insight with me. Sometimes, he said, these thefts are orchestrated to cover up deeper, more complex crimes."

A hush fell over the room. It was Ellie who finally said, "What kind of deeper crimes?" she asked, her voice barely above a whisper.

"Well," Mr. Finch continued, "Stonington suggested that in some cases, the artwork itself might not be the real target at all. Instead, it could be a means of money laundering or other means of hiding large amounts of cash."

Angie's brow furrowed in confusion. "Money laundering? How would that work with stolen art?"

Jenna, always quick to connect the dots, spoke up. "I think I see. If you steal a valuable painting and then sell it on the black market, you've essentially turned a traceable asset – the painting – into untraceable cash. Is that right, Mr. Finch?"

The older man nodded approvingly. "Precisely, Miss Jenna. Of course, Stonington pointed out that this is all speculation at this point. We shouldn't jump to conclusions, or they will lead us down the wrong path."

"Still," Courtney mused, "it's certainly food for thought. It makes the whole case seem even more complicated than before."

Angie stood up, gently depositing Euclid on the warm spot she left behind in the chair. "I think we need to do some more research," she said decisively.

The next few hours were a flurry of activity. Laptops were opened, books were consulted, and the air was filled with the sound of furious typing and the occasional exclamation as someone uncovered an interesting tidbit of information.

Jenna focused on researching the history of the stolen paintings, tracing their provenance as far back as she could. Courtney delved into the backgrounds of the Harringtons, looking for any connections or inconsistencies that might shed light on the case. Ellie, with her knack for numbers, pored over financial records and stock market data, trying to make sense of Mr. Harrington's investment strategies.

As for Angie, she found herself drawn to images of the stolen artworks. There was something about one painting in particular – a small Renoir – that kept catching her attention. She couldn't quite put her finger on it, but every time she looked at the image, she felt a strange tingle of intuition.

"Hey, everyone," she called out, breaking the concentrated silence that had fallen over the room, "can you come look at this for a second?"

The others gathered around Angie's laptop, peering at the image on the screen. It showed a serene Dutch landscape with a windmill silhouetted against a stormy sky.

"What is it, Angie?" Ellie asked, squinting at the picture. "Did you find something?"

Angie shook her head, frustration evident in her voice. "I'm not sure. It's just... there's something about this painting."

Courtney leaned in closer, her nose almost touching the screen. "It looks like a normal painting to me. Beautiful, sure, but normal."

"I know." Angie sighed. "But my intuition is practically screaming at me. Maybe this painting was special to the Harringtons."

Mr. Finch's eyes lit up with interest. "That could be."

Jenna said, "Your intuition has never steered us wrong before. If you think there's something special about this painting, then I believe it."

"Me too," Ellie chimed in. "The question is, how do we figure out what it is?"

As if in answer to Ellie's question, Euclid suddenly leapt onto the desk, landing squarely on the keyboard of Angie's laptop. The screen flickered, and suddenly the image of the Renoir was zoomed in to an extreme close-up of the windmill.

Angie said, "This painting is special to the Harringtons. Its loss is more personal to them."

As the sisters continued to examine the image, each lost in their own thoughts, Angie couldn't help but feel a mix of excitement and apprehension. She had stumbled on something important – she was sure of it, but she also had a feeling this theft was just the tip of the iceberg.

As she looked around at her family, all bent over the laptop in deep concentration, the clock on the mantel chimed midnight, startling them all. They had been so engrossed in their discovery that they hadn't noticed the hours slipping by.

"We should probably call it a night," Ellie said, stifling a yawn. "We can pick this up again in the morning with fresh eyes."

The others nodded in agreement.

As Angie climbed into bed that night and snuggled next to her husband with Euclid and Circe curling up at their feet, her mind was racing with possibilities.

With questions swirling in her mind, Angie drifted off to sleep, her dreams filled with windmills and the promise of adventure that lay ahead.

4

The morning sunlight streamed through the tall windows of the Harrington mansion's library and shined across the antique Persian carpet. Angie sat in a high-backed leather chair, while Chief Martin sat in an upholstered chair near the fireplace, his notebook open. Across from them, Lincoln Harrington, a distinguished gentleman of seventy-nine, settled into his favorite armchair.

Despite his evident wealth, Mr. Harrington had a gentle, unpretentious manner about him. His silver hair was neatly combed, and he wore a cardigan sweater over a crisp blue Oxford shirt. His hands, spotted with age but still steady, rested on the arms of his chair. The only sign of his distress was the slight tremor in his voice when he spoke.

"Thank you both for coming," he said, gesturing to a silver tea service on the side table. "Would either of you care for some tea?"

"No, thank you, Mr. Harrington," Chief Martin replied. "If you don't mind, we'd like to ask you a few questions about the night of the theft."

Angie noted how the older man's shoulders tensed slightly at the mention of the robbery, though he maintained his composure. She could sense waves of distress and confusion coming from him, confirming her intuition that he had no part in the theft.

"Of course." Mr. Harrington nodded. "Anything to help."

"Could you walk us through your evening?" the chief asked, pen poised over his notebook.

Mr. Harrington's blue eyes grew distant as he recalled the events. "It was a rather ordinary evening, really. With Rose in the hospital, I was on my own. I watched a fascinating documentary about World War II on television." He smiled slightly. "History has always been a passion of mine. After that, I read a few chapters of my current book—a crime novel, ironically enough."

"What time did you go to bed?" Chief Martin inquired.

"Around eleven-thirty, after my usual nighttime routine. I always have a cup of decaf tea and one cookie before bed. Rose usually scolds me about the cookie," he added with a sad smile. "I missed her fussing over me."

Angie leaned forward slightly. "Mr. Harrington, where do you typically keep your personal items at night?"

"Oh, I'm quite organized about that," he replied. "My wallet, hearing aid, and reading glasses all go on my bedside night stand. Always in the same spot—force of habit, you understand."

"And you didn't hear anything during the night?" the chief pressed gently.

Mr. Harrington chuckled, though there was little humor in it. "My dear wife jokes that I could sleep through a four-alarm fire. I'm afraid it's true—I heard absolutely nothing. I slept straight through until early morning."

"What about your glasses when you woke up?" Angie asked, remembering the detail from the security footage.

A shadow crossed Mr. Harrington's face. "That's what first alerted me that something was wrong. My reading glasses and hearing aid were on the floor—most unusual. As I was processing that, I noticed my wallet had been tossed a few feet away." His hands gripped the arms of his chair more tightly. "The cash was gone, though they left the credit cards. That's when my heart really started racing."

He paused, taking a deep breath before continuing. "Then I saw the empty space on the wall where the painting had hung. I hurried downstairs to the living room, and when I saw that one of the Dürers was missing as well... well, that's when I called the police."

"And it was only when the police arrived that you discovered the full extent of the theft?" Chief Martin questioned.

"Yes." Mr. Harrington nodded, his voice growing hoarse. "The officer and I went room to room, and I pointed out what was missing. Even now, I can hardly believe it happened."

Angie exchanged a glance with the chief before asking her next question. "Mr. Harrington, who knew about your wife's surgery?"

"Our children, of course—we have two daughters—and several of our friends." He listed a few names, which the chief carefully noted down.

"Had there been any recent disagreements with anyone?" the chief inquired. "Any threats against you or your wife, perhaps?"

Mr. Harrington shook his head emphatically. "Nothing of the sort. We've been blessed with wonderful friendships and a peaceful life."

"Have you ever opened your home to the public?" Angie asked, thinking about potential casing opportunities.

"Ah, yes." Mr. Harrington brightened slightly. "We participated in the holiday open house last year to benefit the preservation society. It's a lovely tradition—the society organizes it along with the historical society. We opened the living room, dining room, kitchen, and sunroom to visitors to see the holiday decorations." He quickly added, "Though we did remove the valuable artwork beforehand, naturally."

Angie nodded, impressed by their precautions. "When will Mrs. Harrington return home?"

"Tomorrow morning," he replied. "She had knee surgery—her meniscus. She'll need to use a cane for a while, but the doctors say she should recover fully."

The chief made a note before asking, "Does your wife know about the theft?"

Lincoln's face fell, and Angie's heart ached at the pain she saw there. "No," he said quietly. "I'm planning to tell her when I visit this afternoon. She's going to be devastated."

"Was one of the paintings particularly special to her?" Angie asked gently, noting the emotion in his voice.

"The Renoir," he replied, his voice thick with emotion. "Rose purchased it before we were married. She developed a love of fine art when she was quite young, and she shared that passion with me. Every time she walked past that painting, her face would light up..." He trailed off, dabbing at his eyes with a handkerchief. "Because of her love for that painting, we became collectors."

Angie felt a wave of sympathy for the older couple. Beyond the monetary value of the stolen paintings, there was clearly a deep emotional attachment to these works of art.

"I'm so sorry," she said softly. "That must make this even harder."

Mr. Harrington composed himself, straightening in his chair. "The worst part is telling Rose. She's always been stronger than me, but this... this will break her heart."

The chief closed his notebook, sensing that Mr. Harrington had shared all he could. "Thank you for your time, sir. We'll do everything we can to recover your paintings."

As they stood to leave, Mr. Harrington walked them to the library door. "Thank you both," he said. "Rose and I have spent forty years building this collection together. Each piece tells a story, holds a memory. They're more than just valuable paintings to us—they're part of our life together."

Outside in the bright morning sun, Angie turned to Chief Martin. "He's telling the truth," she said quietly. "I could sense it. The pain and confusion are real."

The chief nodded. "I agree, which means we need to look elsewhere for our answers." He glanced at his watch. "Let's head back to the station. I want to review the security footage again, particularly around the time Mr. Harrington said he went to bed."

As they walked to their cars, Angie couldn't shake the image of Mr. Harrington's face when he spoke about telling his wife about the theft. Whatever secrets lay behind this robbery, she hoped they'd be able to help solve it—not just for justice, but for the sake of this couple whose precious memories had been stolen along with their art.

A spring breeze rustled through the trees lining the driveway, carrying with it the salty tang of the nearby ocean. Somewhere in Sweet Cove, Angie knew, the stolen paintings were waiting to be found, and with the help of her sisters, Mr. Finch, Chief Martin, and Mr. Finch's mysterious friend Brooks Stonington, she would do what she could to find them.

The afternoon sun filtered through the hospital window, sending warm light across the private room where Rose Putnam Harrington sat in a comfortable chair beside her bed. At seventy-eight, she carried herself well, with her silver-blonde hair neatly styled despite her hospital stay. She had changed out of her hospital gown into a soft blue cashmere sweater and dark slacks, having just returned from her physical therapy session.

Angie noticed the slight grimace of discomfort that crossed Mrs. Harrington's face as she adjusted her position in the chair, though the older woman quickly masked it with a welcoming smile.

"My husband told me you'd be coming by," Rose said, her voice warm but tired. She gestured to the chairs near her. "Please, sit down. I must say, I'm quite ready to go home. Everyone here has been wonderful—very helpful and knowledgeable—but there's nothing like the quiet of one's own home once surgery is done."

Chief Martin settled into one of the visitor chairs, his notebook ready. "You spoke with your husband today?" he asked gently.

Rose's composed expression wavered slightly. "Yes," she said, slowly shaking her head. "Lincoln told me the awful news." She paused, collecting herself. "I'm most grateful that Lincoln wasn't hurt during the robbery, but my goodness..." Her voice caught. "We collected those paintings over decades. Each one holds such precious memories for us."

She looked out the window for a moment, gathering her thoughts. "I keep thinking about those people in our home, going through our things. It feels like such a violation." Her voice grew stronger, touched with indignation. "Lincoln and I have devoted ourselves to donating money and caring for our community. This feels like a slap in the face."

Angie leaned forward, her natural empathy showing in her voice. "Robbers don't care anything about the people they hurt," she said gently. "But please remember, these people aren't part of our community. They severed those ties the moment they decided to invest in a life of crime. Your true community appreciates everything you and your husband do to make life better."

Rose dabbed at her eyes with a delicate handkerchief. "Thank you for saying that. I truly appreciate it."

The chief cleared his throat softly. "Mrs. Harrington, I have to ask some questions that may seem like prying, but they're things I need to know about."

"I understand completely." Rose nodded, straightening in her chair.

"Have there been any arguments or disagreements with anyone recently?"

"No, none at all." Rose shook her head definitively.

"Have you had any workmen at the house?"

Rose started to shake her head again, then stopped. "Well, yes, we have," she amended. "There was an electrical problem in the dining room, and we had an electrician come out."

"When was that?" The chief's pen hovered over his notebook.

"A couple of months ago, I believe." Rose's brow furrowed in concentration.

"Do you recall the electrician's name?"

"Yes, actually." Rose provided the name and

contact information she had stored in her phone, then looked worried. "You don't suppose he had anything to do with the robbery?"

The chief offered a reassuring smile. "Probably not, but we have to follow every lead and suggestion. It's simply protocol."

Angie watched as Rose's hands twisted the handkerchief in her lap. "We understand one of your favorite pieces was taken," she said softly.

Rose's eyes welled up again. "Yes, it was. I purchased that painting so long ago. I loved it so much." She dabbed at her eyes, careful not to disturb her makeup.

"Was there anyone who showed particular interest in the painting?" Angie asked.

"Not that I recall," Rose replied after a moment's thought.

The chief made a note before asking, "Can you tell us who knew you were having surgery?"

"Our daughters and their husbands, my sister, and a few close friends." Suddenly, Rose's eyes widened in dismay. "You don't suspect one of them could be involved? They wouldn't do anything of the sort."

"Please don't worry," the chief assured her quickly. "As I mentioned, some questions are protocol and have to be asked even though they seem very personal or unlikely."

Angie noticed a physical therapy assistant passing by the door and waited until they were gone before asking, "Do you have regular household help?"

"We do," Rose confirmed. "We have a cook who comes three times a week. We also employ a gardening and landscape service, and we have a housekeeper who works a few hours Monday through Friday."

"Did they know you'd be in the hospital?"

"The cook and the housekeeper knew, yes." Rose's voice grew firm. "They're both very nice people and would never have anything to do with the robbery. Maria, our cook, has been with us for fifteen years, and Sarah, our housekeeper, for twelve."

"That's good to know." The chief nodded, making additional notes.

After a few more questions, they could see that Rose was tiring, though she maintained her gracious demeanor. The chief closed his notebook and stood.

"Thank you for your time, Mrs. Harrington," he said. "We may need to get back in touch with you in the future if we have any additional questions."

"Of course," Rose replied. "Anything to help recover our paintings." Her voice caught slightly on the word 'paintings.'

Angie stepped forward and gently touched the older woman's hand. "Try to rest and focus on your recovery. We'll do everything we can to solve this case."

As they walked down the hospital corridor toward the elevator, Angie turned to the chief. "She's telling the truth," she said quietly. "I could sense her genuine distress and shock."

Chief Martin nodded in agreement. "Yes, I believe both Mr. and Mrs. Harrington are completely innocent in this. Their pain is real." He pressed the elevator button. "That means we need to look elsewhere for our answers."

The elevator doors opened with a soft ding, and they stepped inside. As they descended to the lobby, Angie's mind was thinking over the interviews. The Harringtons might not be involved in the theft, but someone in their circle knew about Mrs. Harrington's surgery; someone who knew the layout of the house, the value of the paintings, and most importantly, that Mr. Harrington was a notoriously sound sleeper.

The question was, who was it?

As they emerged into the bright afternoon sunlight, Angie knew she needed to share everything they'd learned with her sisters and Mr. Finch. Between her own intuition, Jenna's ability to sense things about people, Courtney's keen eye for detail, and Ellie's practical wisdom, they might be able to piece together the clues they'd gathered.

She only hoped they would be able to unravel the mystery.

5

The kitchen of the Victorian mansion was alive with activity as the Roseland sisters and Mr. Finch prepared dinner together. Tantalizing aromas filled the air—garlic and herbs from the simmering pasta sauce Angie was stirring, fresh bread baking in the oven, and the sharp scent of Parmesan cheese that Courtney was grating.

From their elevated perch on top of the refrigerator, Euclid and Circe observed the scene with interest, their tails swishing occasionally when a particularly appealing scent wafted their way. The late afternoon sun streamed through the kitchen windows and lit up the organized chaos of meal preparation.

Four-year-old cousins Gigi and Libby sat at the small play table in the corner of the kitchen, thoroughly engaged in "cooking" with their toy pots and plastic vegetables. Their giggles and chatter provided a sweet background melody to the adult conversation.

"More sauce, Mommy!" Gigi called out, pretending to stir an empty pot with great concentration.

Angie smiled at her daughter. "That's right, sweetie. Keep stirring just like Mommy."

Jenna, chopping fresh basil at the counter, glanced at her own daughter Libby, who was carefully arranging plastic carrots in neat rows. "They're going to be master chefs before we know it."

Mr. Finch, seated at the kitchen island, where he was tearing lettuce for the salad, chuckled warmly. "They certainly come by it honestly, especially with Miss Angie's influence."

Ellie, taking out plates and silverware from the cabinets, paused. "Since we're all together, Angie, tell us what you learned from the Harringtons today. Were you and the chief able to interview both of them?"

Angie reduced the heat to let the sauce simmer.

Harrington being away—maybe there was something else they needed to do that they couldn't do with her in the house."

Mr. Finch nodded slowly. "An interesting theory."

"Mommy, I'm hungry," Gigi announced, abandoning her play cooking to tug at Angie's apron.

"Dinner's almost ready, sweetie," Angie assured her, lifting her daughter up for a quick hug. "Why don't you and Libby help Aunt Ellie set out the napkins?"

As the little girls eagerly took on their new task, supervised by an amused Ellie, Courtney finished the salad with a drizzle of balsamic vinaigrette. "So, what's our next move?" she asked.

"First," Angie said, testing the sauce one last time, "we eat dinner as a family. Then tomorrow, we start digging."

Jenna added the pasta to the now-boiling water. "And don't forget about that strange figure in the security footage—the one who was watching but didn't seem to participate in the theft."

"Yes," Mr. Finch said, his eyes sparking with interest. "I'm particularly curious about that individual. What were they doing there? And why haven't they come forward?"

As they finished preparing the meal, the conversation was full of theories and questions flowing as freely as the iced tea Ellie poured into glasses. Soon, they, Josh, Tom, Rufus, and Jack were all seated around the table, passing dishes and helping the little ones with their plates.

As Angie looked around at her family—her sisters, Mr. Finch, the children, the men, and even the cats who had descended from their perch to wind hopefully around their feet—she felt a surge of happiness. Yes, they had a mystery to solve, but these moments, sharing meals, thoughts, and laughter together were the things that made everything worthwhile.

"The pasta's good!" Libby declared, sauce decorating her chin.

"Very, very good," Gigi agreed solemnly, matching her cousin's enthusiastic, if messy eating style.

The adults laughed, and for a moment, the weight of the investigation lifted.

Euclid and Circe, having given up on begging for food, settled nearby, their watchful eyes never leaving their humans.

The mystery of the stolen paintings was far from being solved, but Angie had a feeling they were on the right track. Tomorrow would bring new leads to follow, new questions to ask, and hopefully new answers.

And sometimes, she knew from experience, the best insights came after sharing a meal with the people you loved most in the world.

6

The morning fog rolled in from the ocean, shrouding Silver Cove in a gauzy mist as Angie and Courtney made their way up the circular driveway of the Whitcomb estate. The imposing Georgian-style mansion, with its symmetrical wings and crisp white trim, sat back from the road behind a pair of ornate iron gates. The meticulously maintained grounds, even half-hidden in the fog, spoke of old money and careful attention to detail.

"I remember this place from the holiday tour a couple of years ago," Courtney said, taking in the perfectly manicured grounds. "Mrs. Whitcomb's Christmas decorations were amazing. Remember how she had that huge tree in the foyer with all the antique ornaments?"

"And the Victorian dollhouse display in her library," Angie added. "The chief said she was reluctant to talk to the police about valuable items missing from her home but agreed to meet with us first since we're part of the community. I guess you being an art gallery owner and me owning a bakery makes us less intimidating."

"Or maybe she just feels more comfortable talking to other women," Courtney suggested. "Some of these old families are very private about their lives."

Before they could ring the bell, the heavy oak door swung open. Margaret Whitcomb, an elegant woman in her sixties with perfectly coiffed silver hair, stood in the doorway. She wore tailored slacks and a cashmere sweater in a soft shade of blue, projecting an air of wealth and refined taste. A strand of perfectly matched pearls gleamed at her throat.

"Angie, Courtney, please come in," she said. "I've set up tea in the conservatory. I hope you don't mind, but I've asked my dear friend Charlotte Pembroke to join us. She was also part of the holiday tour committee."

They followed her through a grand foyer filled with museum-quality antiques and original artwork. Angie noticed that several spots on the walls seemed conspicuously bare, though she kept that observation to herself. The room still bore traces of its holiday grandeur – the massive crystal chandelier that had illuminated the Christmas tree and the broad staircase where carolers had stood singing.

Charlotte Pembroke, a petite woman with shrewd dark eyes, was already seated in the conservatory. The light-filled space overlooked extensive gardens, now ethereal in the morning mist. A silver tea service waited on a delicate Queen Anne table, along with a plate of delicate pastries that Mrs. Whitcomb barely glanced at. The woman introduced the two Roseland sisters to Charlotte.

"I love your businesses," Charlotte told them. "Your bake shop, the art gallery, and the candy shop are such wonderful stores to have in town."

Courtney and Angie thanked the woman and explained their connection to the police. "We, our other two sisters, and a dear friend volunteer for the police. We help with research and do interviews for them. We have a good amount of experience assisting with crimes that happen in our community."

"That's wonderful." Charlotte beamed at them.

"You and your family are so talented and accomplished."

"I understand you want to discuss last year's holiday house tour," Margaret said, pouring tea into bone china cups. "Though I'm not sure how I can help with the unfortunate incident at the Harringtons'."

"It was absolutely dreadful to hear about the theft," Charlotte added, stirring her tea. "Rose must be beside herself."

Courtney accepted the tea with a thank you. "Actually, Mrs. Whitcomb, we're looking into some patterns that might be connected to the theft. Have you noticed anything unusual since the tour? Any items out of place, or some things missing?"

The two older women exchanged a quick glance that spoke volumes. Margaret's hands trembled slightly as she set down the teapot. "I don't know what you mean."

"We're not here in any official capacity," Angie said gently. "We're just trying to help out. If something's happened, you can tell us."

Margaret was quiet for a long moment, staring out at her fog-shrouded garden. Charlotte reached over and patted her friend's hand. "Tell them, Margaret. You're not the only one."

Finally, Margaret sighed. "It started with small things. A Sevres porcelain box that I kept in the library – it had belonged to my great-grandmother. Then a miniature portrait from the hallway side table, a family piece from the 1800s disappeared. I thought I must be misplacing them or maybe the housekeeper moved them." She paused, twisting her pearl necklace. "Then two weeks ago, I noticed my grandmother's Fabergé egg was missing from the display cabinet."

"The one that was featured in the holiday tour brochure?" Courtney asked, remembering the beautiful piece.

"Yes. It's been in my family for generations." Margaret's voice caught. "I... I didn't want to believe it at first."

"Charlotte," Angie turned to Mrs. Pembroke, "you said Mrs. Whitcomb wasn't the only one? What did you mean?"

Charlotte nodded. "The Aldridges lost some valuable first editions from their library, and the Carringtons are missing some rare coins. Everyone has been too embarrassed to report it."

"Did you report any of the missing objects?" Courtney asked Margaret.

"No," she admitted. "I was afraid people would

think I was becoming forgetful." She straightened her shoulders. "But I'm not. After I talked with some friends, I know those pieces were taken."

"Do you all live in Silver Cove?" Courtney asked.

"No, I live in Salem, the Aldridges live here in Silver Cove, and the Carringtons live one town over," Charlotte told her.

"Are you missing any items?" Courtney asked Charlotte.

"No, we aren't, but we also weren't involved in the holiday house tour either."

"When did you first notice things missing?" Angie questioned Margaret, her mind already working on the timeline.

"Shortly after we had some electrical work done. The chandelier in the foyer room needed rewiring." Mrs. Whitcomb frowned. "Come to think of it, the electrician spent a lot of time wandering around, claiming he needed to check other fixtures. He seemed particularly interested in our library."

Angie and Courtney exchanged glances. "Do you remember the company that did the work?"

"Elite Home Services," Mrs. Whitcomb replied. "They're very well-regarded. They do work for most of the older homes in the area. In fact, they've done work for almost everyone on the holiday tour circuit."

Just then, through the conservatory windows, Angie spotted a white van pulling up to the house next door. The Elite Home Services logo was clearly visible on its side.

"Would you be willing to show us where the missing items were kept?" Angie asked carefully. "It might help establish a pattern."

The two older women led them through the house, pointing out where each item had been. In the library, Angie noticed fresh marks on the walls near electrical outlets, and in the hallway, a security camera seemed to have been repositioned, its angle slightly off.

"Mrs. Whitcomb," Angie said, "would you be willing to make a list of everything that's missing? And perhaps you could ask your friends to do the same?"

The older woman hesitated, then nodded. "I suppose it's time to stop pretending nothing's wrong." She went to a nearby desk and removed a small notebook, beginning to write.

While Margaret worked on her list, Charlotte drew Courtney aside. "There's something else," she said quietly. "During the holiday tour, I noticed a man taking photos of more than just the decorations. He seemed particularly interested in the security systems, and the layouts of the houses. When I mentioned it to the historical society they said all the volunteers had been vetted."

Margaret returned with her list. "Here are the items I'm certain are missing. There might be more I haven't noticed yet." Her hand shook slightly as she handed over the paper. "I feel so foolish for not speaking up sooner."

"You have nothing to feel foolish about," Angie assured her. "In fact, you might have just helped us uncover something important."

After promising to keep Margaret updated and assuring her they would be diplomatic, Angie and Courtney left the mansion. As they walked to their car, they watched the Elite Home Services van parked next door.

"Should we warn them?" Courtney asked, nodding toward the neighboring house.

"Not yet," Angie replied. "We need to talk to Chief Martin first. Something bigger is going on here, and if we tip our hand too soon..."

"We might spook whoever's behind it," Courtney finished. "But Angie, if they're casing another house—"

"I know." Angie started the car. "Let's get back to the Victorian. We need to talk to the chief, and someone needs to look into Elite Home Services."

Back at the Victorian, they found Jenna and Ellie in the kitchen with Mr. Finch. The older man was entertaining Gigi and Libby with a puppet show.

"You're back early," Jenna noted, looking up from making tea. "Did Mrs. Whitcomb—" She stopped at the expression on her sisters' faces. "What did you find out?"

"We might have uncovered something interesting," Courtney said, spreading out Mrs. Whitcomb's list on the kitchen table. "Look at these items – they're all small, very valuable, and easy to transport. I wonder if there are more victims who haven't come forward."

"The holiday house tour could be the connection," Angie added. "The docents and the attendees were in homes with a lot of valuable items and collections. The thieves could literally pick and choose their targets."

Mr. Finch gathered the children close, and as Angie and Courtney shared what they'd learned, his expression grew increasingly troubled. "My dears," he said finally, "I believe we need to contact Chief Martin immediately. If what you suspect is true, there may be more homes at risk. It also sounds like they started out small and then progressed to the multi-million-dollar heist at the Harringtons' home."

Angie nodded. "I've already informed the chief about what we learned today. He wants us to focus our attention on the Harringtons' art heist. If we divide our attention, then we'll never get anywhere. Chief Martin has assigned officers to investigate the other cases."

Courtney said, "There's also a services company called Elite Home Services. An electrician from that company has been at several homes where valuable items appear to be missing."

"Interesting. I wonder if the same electrician was assigned to the homes." Mr. Finch rubbed his chin.

"Chief Martin is looking into that, too," Angie reported.

What had started as an investigation into a single art theft was possibly becoming something much larger – and potentially more dangerous.

From their perch on top of the refrigerator, Euclid and Circe watched the discussion with their usual feline intensity, as if they too understood that things were about to get much more complicated.

7

The moon was shining across the Harrington estate as Ellie's van pulled up the winding driveway. The magnificent house looked different after dark – more imposing, with its windows looking like watchful eyes in the moonlight. A cool breeze rustled through the trees, carrying the scent of the ocean mixed with the sweet perfume of night-blooming jasmine. In the distance, an owl called softly, its cry echoing across the darkened grounds.

"The Harringtons said they'd leave the exterior lights on for us," Angie said as they parked near the grand entrance. "I still feel bad about disturbing them so late."

"They seemed eager to help," Courtney reminded her as she helped Mr. Finch get out of the van. "I think they're hoping we'll pick up on something the police might have missed."

"The grounds look so different at night," Jenna observed, gazing at the elaborate gardens now changed by shadow and moonlight. "Almost like a different world."

The front door opened before they could ring the bell, spilling warm light onto the stone steps. Lincoln Harrington stood in the doorway, looking tired. His wife Rose stood just behind him, leaning slightly on a decorative cane, her face drawn with fatigue but her posture straight and strong.

"We can't thank you enough for coming," Mr. Harrington said, ushering them into the foyer. "Rose and I have been sitting up most nights anyway. Sleep doesn't come easily anymore."

Mrs. Harrington nodded, gesturing toward the library. "We've made coffee, and there are some cookies. I find myself baking at odd hours now – anything to keep busy." She managed a small smile. "Though nothing as wonderful as your creations, Angie."

The library, with its wood-paneled walls and leather-bound books, felt smaller and more intimate than during their daytime visit. The empty spaces where paintings had hung seemed to draw their eyes like missing teeth in a familiar smile.

"How are you feeling, Mrs. Harrington?" Ellie asked as they settled into the comfortable chairs. "Is your knee healing well?"

"The physical healing is progressing nicely," Rose replied, unconsciously rubbing her knee. "It's the other wounds that are taking longer to mend. Every time I walk into a room and see those empty walls..." She trailed off, accepting the supportive squeeze her husband gave her hand.

"We've had the security system completely upgraded," Lincoln added, pouring coffee into delicate china cups. "Not that it matters much now. The paintings are gone, and with them, so many memories."

"Tell us about the grounds," Mr. Finch said gently, accepting his coffee. "You've lived here for many years – have you noticed any changes in the neighborhood? New people, perhaps? Any unusual activities?"

The Harringtons exchanged glances.

"Now that you mention it," Rose said slowly, "I've noticed more people using the cliff path lately. It used to be just neighbors walking their dogs, but in the past few months there have been others."

"We assumed it was because of the new housing development going in down the coast," Lincoln added. "More people are discovering our little corner of the world."

After about twenty minutes of conversation, during which the Harringtons shared several small observations, the group prepared to examine the grounds.

"We've turned on all the landscape lighting," Mr. Harrington said, walking them to the sunroom, "and there are some flashlights in the drawer if you need them."

The sisters and Mr. Finch made their way into the sunroom. The broken window had been replaced, but Angie could still feel a lingering sense of violation in the space. Through the wall of windows, the elaborate gardens took on an other-worldly quality in the mix of moonlight and land-scape lighting.

Mr. Harrington opened the sunroom door, and the Roseland family stepped outside. "Good luck."

Stone pathways wound between carefully trimmed topiaries, and a distant fountain's falling water could be heard.

"Let's split up," Jenna suggested, pulling her

sweater closer against the evening chill. “We can cover more ground that way.”

“Let’s stay within sight of each other,” Mr. Finch cautioned, his grip tightening on his cane. “There's safety in numbers, even here.”

They spread out across the vast property, each drawn to different areas. Angie followed the path the thieves had taken from the sunroom, trying to see the night through their eyes. The shadows between the hedges would have provided perfect cover, and the soft grass would have muffled their footsteps.

“The security lights are motion-activated,” Courtney called softly, noticing how the illumination followed their movement. “The robbers must have known exactly where to walk to avoid triggering them.”

Ellie moved toward the helipad, which looked eerily empty in the moonlight. “They came this way first,” she said, her voice carrying clearly in the still night air. “I can almost see them – two figures, moving quickly but cautiously.”

“Were there only two?” Courtney asked, joining her sister. Their footsteps crunched softly on the gravel path.

“Look at the security footage stills,” Ellie pointed to her phone, the blue light illuminating their faces.

"There are two distinct shadows ... and there's something else. Do you feel it? They were afraid."

"They were afraid of being caught," Jenna added, hugging herself against more than just the cold.

Mr. Finch nodded slowly, leaning on his cane as he studied the darkened grounds.

"Do you think they were hired?" Jenna asked, moving closer to the group. A night bird called from somewhere in the darkness, making them all jump slightly.

"It would explain their efficiency," Angie mused, her breath visible in the cool air, "because something about them feels amateurish. But they knew exactly what to take and where to go. If they were hired, someone gave them very specific instructions."

They continued their exploration, moving deeper into the property. The moon disappeared behind clouds, making the shadows between the trees seem darker and more mysterious. As they approached the cliff's edge, they could hear the crash of waves against the rocks below. The salt air grew stronger here, mixed with the earthy scent of woods and wet leaves.

"There's a trail over there," Courtney discovered, pointing to a narrow path that wound into the woods. Her flashlight beam revealed a well-worn trail. "It looks like it gets regular use."

"Hello there!"

The sudden voice made them all jump. A man emerged from the shadows of the tree line, walking a large black Labrador on a leash. The dog's tail wagged in greeting, its collar tags jingling softly in the darkness. The man appeared to be in his early fifties, tall and lean, dressed in khakis and a navy windbreaker for his late-night dog walk.

"I'm sorry if I startled you," he said, holding up his hands apologetically. "I'm Paul Benson. I live three houses down in the gray Colonial."

After they introduced themselves, Paul gestured to his dog. "This is Max. He's a friendly fellow – would you like to say hello?" The Lab was already straining toward them hopefully, and Angie bent to scratch behind his ears.

"Beautiful dog," she commented. "How long have you lived in the neighborhood?"

"Going on fifteen years now," Paul replied, his hand absently patting Max's head. "This trail's been here even longer. It winds through the woods around and behind all the neighboring houses. Walking or running the paths is great exercise, and there are some spectacular ocean viewpoints."

"Do you walk here often at night?" Angie asked, trying to keep her voice casual while studying his face in the dim light.

Paul nodded, shifting his weight slightly. "Almost every evening, weather permitting. Max gets restless if he doesn't get his walk. Lately, though..." He hesitated.

"Lately what?" Jenna prompted gently.

"Well, there's been more activity on the trail. Some new faces. I used to know everyone I met out here."

"Were you out walking on the night of the Harringtons' art theft?" Angie questioned directly.

A shadow crossed Paul's face. "Actually, yes. I saw some men walking through the Harringtons' yard that night. I thought they must be guests, maybe heading to the cliff to look at the ocean. It was a beautiful night, clear skies and a full moon." He shook his head, Max pressing against his leg as if sensing his discomfort. "I didn't suspect anything was wrong until I heard about the break-in the next day."

"Did you contact the police about what you saw?" Angie asked.

Paul shifted uncomfortably, his fingers tightening slightly on Max's leash. "No, I didn't think what I saw would be helpful. It was dark, and I only caught glimpses of them through the trees. I couldn't give any real descriptions."

Mr. Finch asked, his keen eyes studying Paul's face. "Did you encounter anyone else on the trail?"

"I didn't run into anyone else," Paul reported. "Though that's not unusual. Not many people use the trail at night."

"Mr. Benson," Courtney said firmly, "you should really contact Chief Martin of the Sweet Cove Police. He's assisting the Silver Cove Police Department. Even the smallest detail might help complete the bigger picture."

Paul nodded slowly. "You're probably right. I've been feeling guilty about not speaking up." He pulled out his phone and made a note of the police station number that Courtney provided.

After Paul and Max continued their walk, the sisters and Mr. Finch gathered closer together.

"What do you think?" Ellie asked in a low voice.

"He seemed sincere," Jenna observed, "but something feels off about the timing. The thieves must have known about this trail – it would have been their perfect escape route."

"And they'd need to know about the neighborhood habits," Angie added, "like Mr. Harrington being a sound sleeper and when people like Mr. Benson usually walk their dogs."

Mr. Finch rubbed his chin thoughtfully. "I wonder how many other neighbors might have seen something that night but haven't come forward."

They spent another hour exploring the property, paying particular attention to the area around the trail. The path was wide enough for several people walking abreast and well-maintained despite its secluded nature.

"Look at this," Courtney called, shining her phone's flashlight on the ground near a bend in the trail. "Cigarette butts. Recent ones."

"The Harringtons don't smoke," Angie remembered from their earlier interviews.

"Someone might have been watching the house," Jenna concluded. "Maybe for several nights, learning the patterns of the neighborhood."

A cool breeze swept up from the ocean, carrying with it a sense of unease. The sisters and Mr. Finch exchanged looks, each feeling there was a whole lot more to uncover to understand the scope of what they were dealing with.

~

Back at the Victorian, over cups of hot chocolate in the warmth of their kitchen, they began dissecting what they'd learned.

"What strikes me about Paul Benson," Courtney said, wrapping her hands around her mug, "is how he seemed like he didn't want to get involved."

"And did you notice how Max kept looking back toward the woods?" Jenna added. "Dogs are sensitive to a person's presence. Someone else might have been out there walking ... or watching us."

"Although I think the thieves might have been amateurs, but they could have been professionals," Mr. Finch mused. "They could have been working for someone else, or it was someone who knew the layout of the house, the neighborhood, and the Harringtons' habits."

"And it was someone who knew exactly which paintings to take," Angie finished. "Was it someone the Harringtons knew, or was it someone who used the holiday tour and Elite Home Services to gain access?"

They talked late into the night, adding their new observations to their growing case file. The pieces were there – the trail through the woods which provided easy access, the strategic timing of the theft, and the careful surveillance beforehand. Now they just had to figure out how they all fit together.

As they finally headed to bed, Angie paused at her window, looking out at the moonlit town. Somewhere out there, perhaps not far away, the people who had orchestrated this theft might be planning their next move. The mystery was deepening, but with each new piece of information, she, her sisters, and Mr. Finch would get closer to uncovering the truth.

8

The morning train to Boston wound its way along the coast, offering glimpses of the ocean between the budding spring trees. Inside the comfortable passenger car, the Roseland sisters and Mr. Finch had found seats together near a window. Around them, business commuters tapped on laptops while a group of college students chatted quietly about an upcoming final exam. The gentle rhythm of the rails and the soft morning light created a peaceful atmosphere for Mr. Finch to tell the sisters more about his old friend.

"Brooks Stonington," Mr. Finch began, settling back in his seat with a contented smile, "is quite a remarkable man. We met when we were both barely out of school, working at Hartley's Art Gallery on

Newbury Street. Those were different times then – Boston was changing and the art scene was evolving."

"That was quite a while ago," Courtney teased gently, making the older man chuckle.

"Indeed, it was, my dear. Brooks was already showing his business acumen even then. While most of us were just happy to be surrounded by beautiful artwork, he was studying the market, learning about valuations and provenance."

"While I became a teacher and stayed informally in the art world," Mr. Finch continued, "Brooks began investing in real estate. He started with a couple of three-family houses in up-and-coming neighborhoods, renting them out and using the income to buy more properties. He had a keen eye for potential. He could walk into a rundown building and see exactly what it could become."

"Like he does with art," Jenna observed, watching a fishing boat cutting through the waves outside their window.

"Exactly." Mr. Finch beamed at her insight. "Brooks never lost his love of art, you see. He studied art history in college while building his real estate empire. Now he owns townhouses in Boston, London, and a beautiful home in Chatham on Cape

Cod, but his true passion has always been art – particularly helping recover stolen pieces."

A train attendant passed through their car, and Ellie purchased coffees for everyone, earning a grateful smile from Mr. Finch as she handed him his cup.

"How did he get involved in art recovery?" she asked, settling back into her seat.

"It started by accident, really. He noticed something odd about a painting at an auction – a small detail in the brushwork that didn't quite match the artist's usual style. Everyone else was ready to bid thousands, but Brooks knew something was wrong. He ended up uncovering a forgery ring. After that, he found he had a knack for tracking down stolen artwork. The right connections, the right knowledge..." Mr. Finch's eyes twinkled. "And perhaps most importantly, the right amount of patience."

"Does he ever work with law enforcement?" Angie asked, thinking about their own collaboration with Chief Martin.

"Yes, he does, though he prefers to work independently. He says there's less red tape that way." Mr. Finch chuckled. "Brooks has always had his own way of doing things."

The train arrived at Back Bay Station thirty

minutes later, the grand architecture of the historic station rising around them as they disembarked. As they emerged onto Dartmouth Street, the city bustled around them. Well-dressed professionals hurried past, briefcases in hand, while tourists consulted maps on their phones. The spring morning had turned warm and bright with cherry trees along the sidewalk dropping pale pink petals in the breeze.

"The city always feels so different from Sweet Cove," Courtney observed as they waited for their taxi. "More intense somehow."

"That's one of the reasons Brooks keeps his place in Chatham," Mr. Finch said. "He says he needs the ocean air to clear his head after too much time in cities."

The Museum of Fine Arts rose before them, its impressive facade gleaming in the late morning sun. Groups of school children filed up the broad steps while art students sketched the building's classical details from the lawn.

"We'll meet him at the café," Mr. Finch directed. "Brooks always says that the museum café has the best coffee in Boston, though I suspect he just likes being surrounded by art while he drinks it."

The café occupied a sun-filled corner of the

museum, its walls adorned with rotating exhibitions of local artists. They found Brooks Stonington already seated at a corner table beneath a vibrant abstract painting, a cup of coffee and a half-eaten scone in front of him. The man radiated energy and sharp intelligence. His silver hair was neatly trimmed, and his casual elegance – from his well-cut blazer to his polished loafers – spoke of wealth worn comfortably. He stood to greet them, embracing Mr. Finch warmly before being introduced to the sisters.

"Victor has told me so much about all of you," Brooks said warmly, gesturing for them to sit. His voice carried traces of a Boston accent, softened by years and travel. "And about your current investigation. A Renoir, two Dürers, a Pissaro, and a Monet – quite a sophisticated heist. The thieves knew exactly what they were after, didn't they?"

After they'd ordered coffee and pastries – Brooks insisting they try the café's famous almond croissants – he leaned forward, his expression growing more serious. "Before we discuss your case, let me tell you about a recent recovery I worked on. It might help you understand how these things often play out in unexpected ways."

The sisters looked eagerly at him.

"The case involved a Cézanne," Brooks began,

breaking off a piece of his scone. "It had been stolen from a collector in central Massachusetts who planned to donate it to a museum. Everyone assumed it had been taken out of the country immediately – that's the usual pattern with high-value pieces."

"But it wasn't?" Angie asked, wrapping her hands around her coffee cup.

Brooks' eyes twinkled. "No, and the way I found it was rather extraordinary. I was shopping online for a birthday gift for my granddaughter when I noticed the painting's image on decorative throw pillows being sold through a home décor website."

"Throw pillows?" Jenna asked incredulously. "Someone was putting a stolen Cézanne on pillows?"

"Not knowingly," Brooks explained. "I followed the metadata trail from the online listing and found it led to an art gallery run by an old acquaintance in Hartford. When I contacted him, he explained he'd photographed the painting at an exhibition in Paris and used the image to emboss various decorative items. He had no idea the painting had been stolen after that exhibition."

"And he was able to help track it down?" Courtney leaned forward, fascinated.

"He told me who had loaned the painting to the exhibition. From there, it was like following bread-crumbs – each person leading to another connection until we finally located the painting in a private collection in Montreal. The collector had purchased it in good faith, having no idea it was stolen."

"That's incredible," Angie said. "How long did it take?"

"Nearly eight months," Brooks replied, signaling a server for more coffee. "And that's actually quite quick for art recovery. These cases often take years, or decades, to resolve, which brings me to some advice for your current situation." He paused as fresh coffee was poured, then continued, "You need to focus your attention on either recovering the paintings or finding the thieves. You can't effectively do both at once."

"In your experience," Ellie asked, "which approach tends to be more successful?"

Brooks considered this as he stirred a bit of sugar into his coffee. "It depends on the circumstances, but in this case, given what Victor has told me about the theft, I'd focus on the paintings. Thieves like these tend to disappear quickly, but the artwork ... art always leaves traces."

"If you decide to focus on the paintings," Brooks

continued, "concentrate on finding just one. They've almost certainly been separated by now – it's safer for the thieves that way. Each painting will follow its own path to its intended destination."

"Intended destination?" Courtney questioned. "You think these weren't just stolen on speculation?"

Brooks shook his head firmly. "Thievery like this usually has specific buyers already lined up. It's too risky otherwise – these aren't pieces you can just walk into a pawn shop with." He paused, watching a group of art students sketch in the museum's courtyard. "And I may have a lead that could help you start tracking them."

"What kind of lead?" Angie looked closely at the man.

"The Brimfield Flea Market opens in a few days. It's only about fifty minutes from here. Most people think of it as just a giant antiques fair, but there's always been a shadowy side to the antiques trade." Brooks lowered his voice slightly. "There's a man there named Marty Martin who runs a booth in the Central Field. He specializes in art prints and frames, but his real specialty is information."

Mr. Finch nodded knowingly. "Ah yes, Marty. I remember him from the old days. He always seemed to know which private collections were buying and selling."

"Exactly," Brooks agreed. "Tell him I sent you. He has his ear to the ground about certain things and might be able to point you in the right direction, but be careful – Marty can be... mercurial. He'll only help if he trusts you."

"Any advice about approaching him?" Jenna asked.

"Be honest about why you're there but don't mention law enforcement. And whatever you do, don't try to haggle with him over his merchandise – he uses those transactions to judge character. If he knows anything about this particular case, I think he'll be helpful once you mention my name."

They spent another hour discussing the intricacies of art theft and recovery, with Brooks sharing stories from his years of experience. He told them about paintings found rolled up in attics, hidden in false walls, and one being used as a tabletop in a remote hunting cabin.

As they prepared to leave, Brooks pulled a small leather notebook from his jacket pocket and wrote down several names and numbers. "These are some contacts who might also be helpful," he said, tearing out the page and handing it to Angie.

"Gallery owners, auction house specialists, and a few private collectors who keep their ears open. Tell them I sent you, and please, keep me updated on your progress. This case... there's something intriguing about it."

"What do you mean?" Ellie asked.

Brooks' expression grew thoughtful. "The combination of paintings taken, the timing, and the execution ... nothing I can put my finger on yet, but..." He shrugged. "Just be careful, and call me if you need anything else."

On the train ride back to Sweet Cove, the sisters and Mr. Finch found a quiet car where they could discuss everything they'd learned. The afternoon sun sparkled on the ocean waves outside their window as they reviewed Brooks' list of contacts.

"I think we should focus on finding the paintings," Jenna said, studying the names Brooks had provided. "The thieves are probably long gone, but the artwork has to surface somewhere eventually."

"The Brimfield market lead sounds promising," Courtney added, pulling up information about the market on her phone. "We were there years ago, but I don't remember it being so huge. There are multiple fields and thousands of vendors. Even if Marty Martin doesn't know anything about our specific paintings, he might know who to ask or where to look."

"It says here the market opens at dawn," Ellie noted, reading over her sister's shoulder. "We should get there early if we want to find his booth before the crowds arrive."

"Brooks seemed to think the paintings would be separated," Angie mused, gazing out the window. "That makes sense – it would be too risky to try selling them all at once. But which one do we focus on first?"

"The Renoir," Mr. Finch suggested quietly, "because it meant the most to Mrs. Harrington."

They spent the rest of the journey planning their trip to Brimfield, with Mr. Finch sharing his memories of previous visits to the massive market. "It's like a small city that appears overnight," he explained. "You'll need comfortable shoes and a good map. And patience – lots of patience."

Back at the Victorian, they gathered in the kitchen to update their case notes while Angie prepared a light dinner for the family. The familiar comfort of home helped them organize their thoughts as they added the new information to their growing file.

"Brooks gave us something else to consider,"

Courtney said suddenly, pausing in making a salad. “Did you notice how he emphasized that these kinds of thefts usually have a specific buyer? That means someone local might know who's been asking about these particular paintings.”

“The art community isn't that large,” Jenna agreed, taking plates out of the cabinets, “especially for works of this caliber. Maybe we should look into recent auctions or exhibitions that featured similar pieces.”

“I can check our gallery's records,” Courtney offered. “See if anyone's been showing special interest in any particular artists lately.”

“And I'll contact some of these names Brooks gave us,” Angie added, stirring a pot of soup. “But first thing tomorrow, we should call Chief Martin. He needs to know what we learned and what we’re going to do next.”

As everyone gathered to eat dinner, the conversation continued to flow as they told their husbands about the trip to Boston, and discussed pieces of the puzzle slowly starting to come together ... the holiday house tour, Elite Home Services, the neighbor who saw the thieves walking across the Harringtons’ lawn, and now the possibility of a specific buyer.

Somewhere in all of this they might find the key to finding the stolen paintings.

"You know what strikes me?" Ellie said thoughtfully, breaking off a piece of bread. "Everything about this feels carefully orchestrated. The timing of Mrs. Harrington's surgery, the thieves, and the targeted selection of paintings... someone spent months planning this."

"Which means they might have spent months planning what happens next," Jenna added. "Where the paintings would go, how they'd be moved..."

"All the more reason to start at Brimfield," Mr. Finch said firmly. "In my experience, even the most carefully planned operations have weak points. Someone always talks, and someone always sees something."

As the evening drew to a close, they finalized their plans for the flea market visit. They would leave early, taking two cars in case they needed to split up. Angie would prepare some of her special muffins for the journey – stake-outs were always better with snacks, she insisted.

Brooks had given them not just leads to follow, but a clearer understanding of what they were dealing with. Someone had planned this theft;

someone who knew exactly what they wanted and how to get it.

Would finding the paintings lead them to the thieves, or would investigating the thieves help them recover the paintings? Despite Brooks' advice to focus on one or the other, Angie had a feeling that in this case, the two paths might turn out to be one and the same.

And maybe, just maybe, they'd find more than they were looking for at the Brimfield Flea Market.

9

The spring morning was cool and bright as Angie and Courtney climbed into Chief Martin's car for the drive to Silver Cove. The chief had arranged to meet James Wilson, an electrician, at the Lighthouse Café, a cozy spot overlooking the harbor, where fishing boats bobbed gently in the morning tide.

"There's something I wanted to mention before we meet Wilson," the chief said as they drove through Sweet Cove's quiet streets. "We've been analyzing the Harringtons' security footage more carefully, and something stands out. The thieves helped themselves to food from the Harringtons' refrigerator and drank from their liquor cabinet."

"That seems very odd. It makes them seem like

amateurs," Courtney noted, exchanging glances with Angie in the back seat.

"Exactly," the chief agreed, turning onto the coastal road. "Professional art thieves don't typically stop for snacks and booze during a heist. They get in, take what they want, and get out. This behavior points to amateurs, or at least to someone comfortable enough in the space to take their time."

"That's interesting," Angie noted. "Maybe the daughters or a friend are involved?"

"A visit from you two will be helpful. They might slip up when talking to you because their guard is down, and you might be able to pick up something from them."

Courtney nodded. "We're looking forward to talk with them."

The Lighthouse Café sat on a small promontory, its weathered shingles and white trim typical of the New England coast. Inside, morning sunlight streamed through large windows, and the aroma of coffee and fresh-baked muffins filled the air. A few early customers sat at tables, most of them appearing to be locals starting their day.

James Wilson was easy to spot. In his mid-thirties, he was wearing a neat polo shirt with his company's logo. He stood to greet them, his handshake firm and professional.

After ordering coffees and pastries, they settled at a corner table overlooking the harbor. Up close, James had an earnest face and careful manner that spoke of someone who took pride in his work.

"Thank you for meeting us," Chief Martin began. "I know you must be busy with jobs."

"Not a problem," James replied. "Always happy to help if I can. Though I have to say, I was surprised to get your call." He glanced at the sisters, then back to the chief.

"You must have heard about the recent break-ins?" the chief asked.

"I have, yeah."

The chief kept his tone carefully neutral. "We understand you did work at some of the houses involved."

James nodded, wrapping his hands around his coffee mug. "I did, including the Harrington place. It's awful what happened to them."

"How did you get those jobs?" Angie asked gently. "Did the homeowners contact you directly through your own business?"

"Some did. Word of mouth is still the best advertising in this business." James took a sip of his coffee. "Other jobs I get through Elite Home Services."

"Can you tell us about Elite?" Angie leaned forward slightly, noting how James's expression remained open and earnest.

"It's a national brand. They offer reliable services to homeowners and businesses." He gestured to his polo shirt with its embroidered logo. "All the workers are vetted – background checks, references, the whole thing. They keep a portion of the fee, and the rest goes to us contractors. It's a way of expanding our business opportunities."

"You don't work exclusively for them?" Courtney asked.

James shook his head. "Some people do, but I just take jobs when I have the time. I prefer having my own business, but Elite brings in good supplemental work."

"Let's talk specifically about the Harrington house," the chief said. "Can you walk us through the work you did there?"

"Sure. There was an electrical problem that needed attention - flickering lights and some voltage issues." James reached for his phone and pulled up his work order. "Here's the original service request. The main issue was the dining room chandelier."

"What parts of the house did you need to access?" Courtney asked, noting his methodical approach to answering questions.

"I was in the dining room mostly, working on the chandelier. I had to spend some time in the basement too, checking the electrical panel." James paused, considering. "I also went into the living room and sunroom. Mrs. Harrington was actually in the sunroom the whole time, doing some paperwork."

"Why did you need to go into the living room?" the chief questioned, his pen poised over his notebook.

James leaned back slightly. "It's an older house. Sometimes the wiring can be complicated. Previous owners might have done their own work and created unusual circuits. I checked the living room to trace where the power issues might be originating from." He shrugged. "The living room wiring seemed okay for now, but I told Mrs. Harrington to call right away if anything started acting up. Houses this age often need complete rewiring eventually."

The chief took a sip of his coffee before asking, "Where were you on the night of the Harrington break-in?"

"I was in Chicago," James replied without hesitation. "My mother's been having some health issues. My sister and I take turns going out there to help out and check on her." He pulled out his phone again. "I still have my plane tickets and receipts if you need to see them."

When the chief asked about his whereabouts during the other break-ins, James had the same answer - Chicago. His timeline checked out perfectly.

"Did anyone ask you about the layout of the Harringtons' house?" the chief's question was casual but direct.

James's eyebrows shot up in surprise. "No. No one has."

"Not even someone from Elite Home Services?"

"Definitely not." James shook his head emphatically. "If they did, I'd be suspicious. I'd wonder why that was any of their business. We're there to do specific jobs, not case houses."

After a few more questions, they wrapped up the interview. James headed off to his first job of the day, leaving the chief and the sisters still at their table.

"What do you think?" the chief asked quietly.

"He's telling the truth," Angie said with certainty. "Every answer was direct and consistent."

"I agree," Courtney added, "and did you notice

how organized he was? The work orders, the receipts - everything documented."

The drive back to Sweet Cove was thoughtful, the three of them thinking over what they'd learned.

"Maybe we can eliminate Elite Home Services as being directly involved," Angie suggested, watching the coastline slip past. "They might be legitimate after all."

"Could be," the chief agreed. "Although someone knew an awful lot about the Harringtons' house and their security system."

"And about the homeowners' schedules," Courtney added. "Like when Mrs. Harrington would be in the hospital."

They discussed their upcoming trip to Brimfield the next day, reviewing what Brooks had told them about Marty Martin and his booth in the Central Field.

"I hope this lead pans out and gives us something to go on," Courtney said. "Finding even one of the paintings might help us trace the others."

The chief pulled up in front of the Victorian, where spring flowers nodded in the sea breeze. "Keep me posted about what you find at Brimfield," he said, "and be careful."

Back inside the Victorian, Angie and Courtney

found Jenna and Ellie preparing for tomorrow's trip, studying maps of the flea market's layout and making lists of questions for Marty Martin.

"How did it go with the electrician?" Jenna asked, looking up from her laptop.

As they shared the details of the interview, Angie had a feeling they might be missing something obvious. The electrician was innocent, but someone had used inside knowledge to plan the art heist ... someone who knew about valuable artwork, household schedules, and security systems.

Who had access to all that information, and how could they find out who it was?

As they continued their preparations for Brimfield, the spring breeze carried the scent of the ocean through the open windows. Hopefully, tomorrow would bring new leads to follow, new questions to ask, and maybe, some answers about the stolen paintings.

10

The early morning sun painted the sky in shades of pink and gold as Ellie's van joined the steady stream of vehicles heading toward Brimfield. The massive flea market was spread across multiple fields, each already bustling with activity as vendors set up their displays. American flags fluttered in the warm spring breeze, and the aroma of coffee and fresh-baked goods floated from food trucks lining the paths.

"I'd forgotten how enormous this place is," Courtney said, gazing out at the sea of white tents and colorful canopies stretching as far as the eye could see. Antique furniture, vintage clothing, rare books, and countless other treasures were being carefully arranged as early shoppers began to browse.

"We haven't been here for a long time." Jenna admired some soft blankets on display.

Mr. Finch, studying the market map they'd downloaded from the internet, pointed toward the Central Field. "Marty Martin's booth should be in that direction. Brooks said he always sets up in the same spot – near the old oak tree at the crossroads."

They made their way through the growing crowds, passing displays of gleaming silver, delicate porcelain, and weathered farm equipment. A woman haggled over a Victorian writing desk while nearby, a collector carefully examined a set of Civil War medals. The paths between booths were already filling with serious buyers pulling wheeled carts and casual browsers simply enjoying the festive atmosphere.

"There's the oak tree." Ellie spotted it first, its massive branches providing welcome shade. Beneath it, a professional-looking booth displayed an impressive collection of artwork and frames. A man in his sixties, wearing wire-rimmed glasses and a canvas apron, was carefully adjusting a painting's position.

"That must be Marty," Angie murmured. "Remember what Brooks said. We should let Mr. Finch take the lead."

They approached the booth, admiring the carefully curated selection of artwork. Marty Martin glanced up at them briefly before returning to his task. His movements were precise and practiced, suggesting years of handling pieces.

"Good morning," he said without looking up. "Browse all you like. Everything's clearly priced."

"Actually," Angie said stepping forward, "we're from Sweet Cove, near the coast."

Mr. Finch added, "We're here about something specific."

"Well, good luck with that." Marty continued adjusting the artwork on his shelves with care. A strand of silver hair fell across his forehead as he worked, and he brushed it back with a quick gesture.

The booth around them was meticulously organized, with prints of paintings arranged by size and style. Antique frames gleamed in the morning sun, their gilt edges catching the light. A few early customers browsed nearby, admiring a collection of maritime scenes.

Moving closer to examine a particularly nice seascape, Courtney said, "Mr. Finch and I own an art gallery in Sweet Cove. We were devastated to hear about the Harrington theft. Such wonderful pieces were taken."

Mr. Finch stepped forward then, his cane tapping softly on the gravel path. “My dear friend Brooks Stonington suggested we speak with you.”

The change in Marty's demeanor was immediate. He straightened up, his sharp eyes focusing on Mr. Finch with new interest. “Brooks, huh? How do you know the old man?”

“We knew each other in our teens.” Mr. Finch smiled warmly. “We worked together at an art gallery in Boston. We've kept in touch over the years. He's a fine man.”“And a very wealthy one.” Marty's expression softened slightly. “He knows what he's doing.” He studied them more carefully now, his earlier dismissive manner replaced with thoughtful consideration. “You're interested in the Harrington heist. Did Brooks give you any clues to follow?”

Mr. Finch smiled gently. “He told us to talk to you.”

A middle-aged woman in a floral sundress approached the booth then, her attention caught by a coastal scene in muted blues and grays. Marty smoothly shifted his attention to her, discussing the artist's technique and history with obvious expertise. His weathered hands carefully wrapped the print after the sale, showing his years of experience handling artwork.

When he returned, Marty positioned himself near Mr. Finch, his voice lowered. Around them, the market had grown busier, with the morning air filled with conversation and laughter as more shoppers arrived. The oak tree's spreading branches provided welcome shade from the strengthening sun.

"I'm sure you know there are networks of people in the art world," he began, adjusting his wire-rimmed glasses. "I've heard some rumblings about the Harrington heist. It wasn't a very sophisticated robbery... which makes people think it was done by amateurs who were hired by someone to do it, or that it was deliberately done in an amateurish way to throw off law enforcement."

He paused to straighten a frame that had tilted slightly. "Those paintings would be moving quickly. Some are probably already out of the country. Those can be very difficult to get back. It can take decades, with lots of legal wrangling back and forth." Drawing a deep breath, he continued, "There may be one or two pieces that are still in the area, but they won't stay here long."

Another customer called out a question about a landscape painting, and Marty excused himself briefly. The sisters exchanged glances while they waited, each noting how different Marty's demeanor had become at the mention of Brooks' name.

When he returned, Marty moved closer to Mr. Finch, his voice even quieter. “There's a couple who run an art gallery nearby. Their names are Beth and Nathan Collins. The gallery is called Collins International Art.” He glanced around before continuing. “They've been traveling in Europe but might be home already. Swing by there and ask about the Harringtons' paintings. Be pleasant. Don't be confrontational. You can tell them I sent you.”

Mr. Finch extended his hand to thank Marty, and as they shook, he felt an unexpected zing rush through his palm. Something about the contact made him pause, though he kept his expression neutral.

As they walked away from the booth, the market had grown even more crowded. Children darted between stalls, clutching vintage toys, while serious collectors huddled in quiet negotiations over rare finds. The aroma of fresh coffee drew them to a red food truck parked near a cluster of picnic tables under maple trees.

“Let's get something to drink and talk this over,” Ellie suggested, already reaching for her wallet.

Armed with steaming coffees and still-warm

pastries, they settled at a shaded table away from the main crowd. A gentle breeze carried the sounds of distant haggling and the upbeat music of a performer's guitar.

"Marty didn't give us a lot of information," Courtney said, breaking her almond croissant in half. A few crumbs scattered on the worn wooden table as she spoke. "But maybe Beth and Nathan Collins will give us something to go on."

"At first, I didn't even think he was going to talk to us." Jenna took a careful bite of her own pastry, brushing flour from her fingers. "He really changed when he heard Brooks' name."

"Marty must have his finger on the pulse of the art network," Angie mused, placing her hands around her coffee cup. "I wonder if he knows more than he's telling."

Ellie reached up to touch her mother's cabochon necklace, a habit she had when thinking deeply. The stone caught the morning light, sending tiny flashes of color across the table. "I think he gave us something we would never have found on our own. Beth and Nathan Collins must have connections that can help us."

"I certainly hope so." Mr. Finch nodded, still looking thoughtful. "We need to move fast before the paintings are out of reach." He flexed his hand slightly, as if still feeling that strange sensation from the handshake. "You know, when I shook with Marty, I felt an electrical pulse pass from his hand to mine."

"What do you think it means?" Courtney asked.

"I'm not sure. It puzzled me. Does the man know more than he's telling us, perhaps, or was his information so important that it gave me a jolt?"

"Maybe we'll need to return to the market to chat with him again," Ellie told them.

They spent another hour exploring the market, though their minds were clearly on their next destination. The fields had filled completely now, creating a temporary city of treasures and trinkets. A woman haggled over a Victorian music box while her husband examined vintage fishing gear. Children begged for cotton candy from a vendor whose cart was festooned with colorful balloons.

"I wish we could stay longer," Courtney said as they made their way back to the van. "Some of these pieces would be perfect for our gallery."

"We can come back another time," Angie assured her. "Right now, we need to focus on finding those paintings."

The van was hot from sitting in the sun, and Ellie

started the engine to get the air conditioning running. As they settled into their seats, Mr. Finch consulted the directions to the Collins International Art Gallery that Marty had provided.

"It's about twenty minutes from here," he reported, studying the map. "It's in one of those old mill buildings that's been converted to shops and galleries."

They pulled out of the crowded parking field, joining the steady stream of cars leaving the outdoor market. Behind them, the white tents and colorful canopies stretched across the rolling fields like a giant patchwork quilt, the morning sun now high in the cloudless sky.

As they drove through the Massachusetts countryside, each was lost in their own thoughts about what they might discover at the Collins gallery. So far, clues had been hard to find, but maybe the owners of the gallery would point them in the right direction.

Angie wondered why Marty Martin had seemed so certain that some of the artwork was still in the area. He was probably just guessing.

The converted mill building came into view, its red brick walls rising impressively against the blue spring sky. A sign directed them to parking at the front of the building, where the rushing sound of the river that once powered the mill provided a constant background melody.

"Collins International Art," Ellie read from a professional bronze plaque beside a heavy glass door. "Well, shall we see what they can tell us?"

"Here's hoping." Jenna nodded and pulled open the gallery door.

11

The Collins International Art Gallery made an impressive statement even from the outside. Housed in the restored mill building, its massive windows had been polished to perfection, reflecting the spring sunlight like mirrors. Through the gleaming glass, elegant track lighting highlighted carefully positioned sculptures and paintings. A brass plaque beside the heavy door announced gallery hours in flowing script.

Inside, the space took full advantage of the mill's industrial history while transforming it into something much more refined. The entire first floor stretched out before them, with soaring ceilings supported by original wooden beams that had been carefully restored to a rich honey color. Sunlight streamed through tall, arched windows, highlighting gleaming hardwood floors and pristine white walls. Modern track lighting supplemented the natural light, creating perfect illumination for the artwork displayed throughout the space.

Near the entrance, a Rodin sculpture caught the light, its bronze surface seeming to move with each shift in perspective. A young assistant in sleek black clothing sat at a minimalist desk, speaking softly into a phone about an upcoming installation.

Beth and Nathan Collins appeared from different directions. Beth, tall and willowy in her early forties, wore a perfectly tailored black Chanel dress and jewelry that probably cost more than most cars. Her dark hair was swept into an elegant chignon, and her red-soled Louboutin shoes clicked precisely on the hardwood floors.

Nathan, slightly older, projected casual wealth in his designer jeans and dove-gray cashmere sweater, with his salt-and-pepper hair artfully tousled in that way that takes a lot of work to appear effortless.

"Welcome to Collins International," Beth greeted them, her smile professional but reserved. Her French manicure looked elegant as she gestured toward a seating area where low white leather chairs surrounded a glass coffee table adorned with art books. "Would you like some coffee? We just received a new shipment of beans from a small plantation in Costa Rica."

Nathan moved to stand slightly apart from his wife, his stance casual but somewhat protective of a certain section of the gallery. "Or perhaps sparkling water? We find many of our clients prefer to refresh themselves while viewing the collections."

Before anyone could respond, Mr. Finch stepped forward, leaning slightly on his cane. "We're here because we're assisting the police with research on the art heist at the Harrington mansion in Silver Cove. Marty Martin from the Brimfield Market suggested we come to see you. My dear friend Brooks Stonington introduced us to Marty."

The change in Beth and Nathan's expressions was subtle but noticeable. Beth's fingers tightened slightly on the tablet she was holding, while Nathan's casual stance became more rigid. A glance passed between them so quickly it might have been imagined.

"Ah, Brooks," Nathan said after a moment, his voice carrying a hint of something that might have been amusement or disdain. "Is he still working? I haven't heard his name mentioned in collecting circles lately."

The condescension in his tone wasn't lost on anyone. Mr. Finch straightened, his usual gentle demeanor taking on an edge of steel. "I'm slightly older than Brooks," he informed Nathan, his voice carrying the weight of years of experience in the art world. "My colleague and I own a candy shop and an art gallery located on Main Street in Sweet Cove. The stores are quite successful, and we're thinking of expanding."

Nathan had the grace to look uncomfortable, though something flickered in his eyes that suggested annoyance. "I didn't mean to imply that Brooks should stop working..."

With a slight smile, Mr. Finch held up his hand. "A discussion for another day. We're looking for information about the artwork taken from the Harrington home and wondered if you had any ideas on the matter."

Beth stepped forward smoothly, clearly trying to ease the tension. "We buy and sell paintings and know quite a few people involved in the international art world. Let me show you some of the work we have on display. Come with me into the next gallery room."

As they followed Beth through an elegant archway, Courtney noticed how Nathan lingered behind slightly, typing something into his phone before following. The next space they entered was even more impressive than the first. Masterworks hung like jewels against the white walls, each piece perfectly lit to enhance its unique qualities.

A Georgia O'Keeffe blazed with desert colors, and beside it hung a dreamy Chagall that seemed to float on the wall, its distinctive style immediately recognizable. A small but exquisite Monet captured a moment of sunlight on water, while a Vermeer drew the eye with its masterful use of light and shadow. A surreal Dali completed the impressive collection, its melting forms creating an unsettling contrast to the more traditional pieces.

"Your collection is remarkable," Courtney said, her professional eye noting both the quality and variety of the works. "The lighting design really brings out the subtle colors in the Monet."

Beth's smile became more genuine at the technical observation. "We had the lighting system specially designed. Each section can be adjusted to the specific needs of different pieces." She moved closer to the Monet. "This one, for instance, needs soft, diffused light to really capture the impressionistic technique."

"You have quite a varied inventory," Jenna noted,

watching as Nathan positioned himself near what appeared to be a door to a back room.

"We travel the world to bring back paintings that we know will please our clients," Beth explained, though her eyes kept darting to her husband. "We just returned from Europe yesterday with some new pieces. The market there is quite active at the moment."

Nathan shifted his weight, and Angie noticed how his hand touched his phone again, as if checking for messages. "Our clients expect us to stay current with international trends," he added, his tone suggesting their visitors might not fully appreciate such matters.

"Have you heard any whisperings about the Harringtons' paintings?" Angie asked directly, observing how Beth's hand moved to her throat, fingering an expensive-looking pendant.

"We hear things," Beth replied carefully, her eyes meeting Nathan's briefly. "But all of it is speculation. All of our inventory is well-documented with a trail of receipts. We never deal in stolen work." She moved toward a smaller Vermeer, as if seeking comfort from its soft scene.

"We've heard you're both well-respected, reliable, and trustworthy," Jenna said smoothly, noting how Nathan's jaw tightened at the word 'trustworthy.'

"That's why we hoped you might be able to point us to someone who may have heard something about the stolen paintings," Ellie added, watching Beth's reflection in the glass covering a small sketch. "Any bit of information could be helpful."

Nathan moved closer to his wife, his designer shoes silent on the polished floor. "At this time, we don't have anything to share, but if we do, we can certainly let you know." His tone suggested the conversation was over.

"Perhaps we could discuss the current market for Impressionist works," Mr. Finch suggested mildly, "given the Monet that was taken from the Harringtons."

"I'm afraid we have an appointment arriving shortly," Beth interrupted, though no other clients were visible in the gallery. "But please, take my card. We'll certainly be in touch if we hear anything useful."

The gallery seemed colder somehow as they said their goodbyes, despite the warm spring sunlight still streaming through the windows. Beth's smile remained fixed and professional, while Nathan barely acknowledged their departure, his attention focused on his phone once again.

In the van, the tension that had been building inside the gallery finally broke.

"I don't trust them," Ellie announced as she backed the van out of the parking space. The sound of the river rushing past the old mill provided a comforting sound, but it didn't soothe Ellie's mood. "Did you notice how Beth kept looking at that door near the Vermeer? And how Nathan wouldn't let anyone get close to it?"

"I sense they know something," Jenna agreed from the backseat, "but they're holding back. Beth started to say something about the European market, but Nathan cut her off."

"I didn't like Nathan at all," Angie shared, shaking her head. "He seems full of himself. He makes me think of a strutting peacock. And did anyone else notice how he kept checking his phone? It was like he was waiting for some important message to come through."

"I think they're trying to put on a show," Courtney said thoughtfully, her gallery experience evident in her comments. "But there's definitely trouble in paradise. I felt like Beth and Nathan weren't getting along. The tension between them was obvious, especially when Beth mentioned their recent European trip."

"Really?" Ellie narrowed her eyes as she navigated onto the main road. "You think there's marriage trouble?"

Courtney shrugged as her expression became thoughtful. "Something about them didn't seem like they were working as partners. I don't know how to explain it, but there was some weird undercurrent. The way Beth would start to say something and he'd cut her off, and how they never quite looked at each other directly. And that comment about the European market being 'active' – Beth seemed almost nervous when she said it."

"Perhaps Nathan will call us at a later date," Mr. Finch surmised, though his tone suggested he didn't really believe it. "The ball is in their court now. Though I must say, their reaction to Brooks' name was rather surprising."

Jenna sighed, watching the old mill building disappear behind them. "I thought we'd have some tiny clue we could bring back to Chief Martin, something concrete to work with. All we have are suspicions and odd behavior."

"There are plenty of people yet to be interviewed," Mr. Finch pointed out, his optimism returning. "We shall remain hopeful, and perhaps..." He paused thoughtfully, "Perhaps what we observed about their behavior is a clue in itself; their anxiety about Brooks and Marty Martin, along with Nathan's protective stance near certain areas of the gallery."

The van fell silent as they all considered this. The Collins gallery had been impressive, certainly, but something about it felt off, like a painting that appeared perfect at first glance but revealed tiny inconsistencies on closer inspection.

Through the rear-view mirror, Ellie caught a glimpse of a sleek black Mercedes emerging from the mill parking lot. "Don't look now," she said quietly, "but I think we're being followed. They must be trying to intimidate us."

As they drove back toward Sweet Cove, the Mercedes maintained a discreet distance, its tinted windows revealing nothing about its occupants.

The mystery of the Harrington paintings was growing more by the day, but as Mr. Finch had suggested, sometimes the most important clues weren't found in what people said, but in what they left unsaid. And the Collins, for all their polish and sophistication, had indeed left quite a lot unsaid.

12

"I always forget how beautiful this place is," Courtney said as she and Mr. Finch climbed the worn stone steps of the historical society. "It's like stepping back in time."

Inside, the foyer's dark woodwork gleamed with generations of polish, and a grandfather clock ticked away in the corner. Martha Whitaker, the society's longtime secretary, greeted them warmly.

"The holiday tour records?" She adjusted her reading glasses. "Of course. We keep everything organized in the research room. Though I must say, it's unusual to have anyone interested in last year's tour at this time."

The research room occupied what had once been the mansion's library. Floor-to-ceiling bookshelves held carefully preserved documents, while a large oak table dominated the center of the room. Sunlight filtered through sheer curtains, dancing across the polished surfaces.

"Here we are," Martha said, placing a couple of boxes on the table. "Everything from last year's tour - volunteer applications, house descriptions, photographs, and even the printed programs."

Mr. Finch settled into one of the carved wooden chairs, his experienced eyes already scanning the materials. "Quite an organized system you have here."

"We try to keep good records." Martha smiled. "Let me know if you need anything else." She left them to their research, her footsteps fading on the hardwood floors.

Courtney and Mr. Finch began methodically sorting through the materials. The volunteer applications were arranged alphabetically, each one filled out in different handwriting styles. Some included local addresses they recognized, and others were from neighboring towns.

"Look at this one," Courtney said after about an hour of searching. She held up an application form filled out in precise block letters. "Donald Prior." She stared at the paper. "I'm feeling some energy from this. Something about it feels ... off."

Mr. Finch adjusted his glasses, studying the paper. "The handwriting is almost too perfect, isn't it? As if someone was trying very hard to write carefully." The man lifted the form and held it for several moments. "I agree. I feel it too. There is something definitely wrong about whoever filled out this form."

They examined the form more closely. Donald Prior had listed his address at 317 Oak Street in the nearby town of Bristol-by-the-Sea, claimed to be a graduate student studying local architecture, and expressed particular interest in historical homes.

"The address is wrong." Courtney pulled out her phone and checked a map. "There is no 317 Oak Street in Bristol. The street numbers only go up to 300."

Mr. Finch's eyebrows rose. "Martha?" he called softly. When the secretary appeared, he asked, "Do you remember a young man named Donald Prior who volunteered for the holiday tour?"

Martha's forehead wrinkled in concentration. "Prior... yes, I do remember him. Tall young man, very polite. He seemed quite knowledgeable about architecture, but you know, I don't recall seeing him after the tour ended. Most of our volunteers stay involved with the society, but he just ... disappeared. I wondered if he moved away."

"Were there any photos taken during the tour?" Courtney asked.

"Oh yes, quite a few. They should be in that blue folder there."

Courtney began flipping through the photographs, most showing festively decorated rooms, smiling homeowners, and tour visitors. Then she stopped, her finger resting on one particular image.

"Mr. Finch, look at this."

The photograph showed the Harringtons' grand foyer decorated for Christmas. In the background, partially turned away from the camera, stood a tall young man in a blazer, apparently discussing something with a tour guest.

"There's another one," Mr. Finch said, pointing to a different photo. This one showed the same man, again from the side, standing near the entrance to the Harringtons' living room.

With slightly trembling fingers, Courtney pulled up the security footage from the Harrington heist on her phone. The grainy nighttime images showed two figures moving through the property. One of them, the tallest, seemed to have a familiar stance.

"The height is right," she whispered, "and the way he carries himself..."

Mr. Finch leaned closer, his eyes narrowing. "The security footage is of such poor quality, but the physical similarities are striking."

They spent another hour comparing the holiday tour photographs with the security footage. In none of the historical society photos was Donald Prior's face clearly visible, but his height, build, and characteristic way of moving seemed to match one of the thieves.

"He used the tour to learn the layout of the Harringtons' house," Courtney realized, "and look at his stance in each photo he's in. He must have kept an eye on the photographer so he could turn away from being photographed straight-on."

"A very clever plan," Mr. Finch agreed. "Join the historical society, volunteer for the holiday tour, and gain access to multiple wealthy homes at once."

"And gather information about security systems, valuable artwork, and homeowners' habits." Courtney carefully photographed Donald Prior's application form and the relevant tour photos with her phone. "We need to show these to Chief Martin."

As they prepared to leave, Martha appeared with a small box. "I just remembered - we also kept copies of the tour guide scripts that each volunteer used. Would you like to see those as well?"

Courtney and Mr. Finch exchanged glances. "Yes, please," they said in unison.

The script assigned to Donald Prior had covered the Harringtons' house. On the margins were small notations in that same precise handwriting - apparently innocent observations about architecture that now seemed far more sinister.

Outside, the spring day had grown warmer, but Courtney felt a chill. "How many other historical societies has he done this to?" she wondered aloud. "How many other towns?"

"That's something for Chief Martin to investigate," Mr. Finch said, patting her arm gently. "But we've found an important piece of the puzzle. Donald Prior may not be his real name, but now we know how he chose his target."

They walked back to Courtney's car, both lost in thought about the young man who had used the seacoast area's cherished holiday tradition for such criminal purposes. But at least now they had a lead - and perhaps, with it, a way to start tracking down the stolen paintings.

The evening sun sent long shadows across the Victorian's front porch as Chief Martin's car pulled into the driveway. Inside, the house was warm and welcoming, filled with the smell of fresh-baked cookies and brewing tea.

Euclid and Circe watched from their usual perch atop a bookshelf as the family settled into the comfortable family room. The cats' eyes followed the chief's movements with their usual intensity, as if they too knew important information was about to be shared.

"These cookies are delicious, Angie," the chief said, accepting a cup of tea from Ellie. "Though I'm afraid my news isn't as pleasant as your baking."

Mr. Finch settled in his favorite armchair. "Before you begin, Phillip, Courtney and I have something to share about our visit to the Historical Society."

They told the chief about Donald Prior's suspicious application and the photographs that seemed to match one of the thieves from the Harringtons' security footage. As they spoke, the chief's expression grew increasingly serious.

"This fits with something else that's happened," he said when they finished. "Mrs. Harrington received a very disturbing phone call this afternoon."

"A phone call?" Angie asked, absently scratching Euclid's ears after the orange cat jumped down to settle in her lap.

The chief set his teacup down carefully. "A man with what Rose Harrington described as an Eastern European accent called her private line. He said he knew where the paintings were." He paused, his expression troubled. "Rose became quite upset during the conversation. The man apparently made some comments about the Renoir - details about the painting that only someone who had seen it up close would know."

Circe's tail swished back and forth as she stared intently at the chief, as if she understood what he was saying.

"Did the caller make any demands?" Jenna asked, sharing a concerned glance with her sisters.

"No, that's the strange part. When Rose asked where the Renoir was, he just hung up. We tried tracing the call, but it came from a burner phone. The only thing we could determine was that it pinged off a cell tower near Brimfield."

"Brimfield?" Courtney straightened in her chair.

"That's quite a coincidence, considering our visits to Marty Martin and the Collins gallery."

"My thoughts exactly," the chief agreed. "The timing of this call, coming right after your investigations in that area, seems significant."

Mr. Finch rubbed his chin thoughtfully. "Perhaps someone is nervous about what we might discover. This could be an attempt to ... what? Warn us off? Or possibly set up some kind of negotiation?"

"But why call Mrs. Harrington directly?" Ellie wondered. "Why not contact the police or the insurance company?"

The chief shook his head. "The insurance company is in the process of paying out on the claim. This feels more personal somehow."

"How is Mrs. Harrington holding up?" Angie asked, concern evident in her voice.

"She's shaken but keeping it together. Lincoln has arranged for additional security at their house, just in case, and as we know, they have upgraded their security system."

The family room fell quiet as they all considered the information. Outside, the evening darkness had deepened, and Ellie rose to draw the curtains. The room felt cozier with the outside world shut away but also somehow more isolated.

"Do you think there's a connection between Donald Prior and this phone call?" Jenna asked finally.

"It seems likely that Prior is involved with the heist somehow," the chief replied. "The timing is too convenient to be coincidental. First you discover Prior's connection to the holiday tour, and then this call comes in from the Brimfield area."

"And let's not forget about Beth and Nathan Collins," Courtney added. "Their gallery isn't far from Brimfield, and they definitely knew more than they were telling us."

Mr. Finch nodded slowly. "The pieces are starting to come together, but I'm not sure I like the picture they're forming. This feels less like a simple theft and more like a carefully orchestrated plan."

"But orchestrated by whom?" Angie wondered aloud. "And why these specific paintings? They must have been taken because of their value."

The chief stood, preparing to leave. "Those are exactly the questions we need to answer. I've put out inquiries about similar cases involving holiday home tours in other towns, and I'm having someone look into Donald Prior's description and method of operation. People like that tend to repeat what works."

"We'll keep digging too," Angie assured him. "It seems we might be getting closer."

As they walked the chief to the door, Euclid and Circe followed, their eyes still fixed on him. The night air was cool and fresh.

"Be careful," the chief warned as he prepared to leave. "If this phone call was meant as a warning, whoever's behind this might not appreciate your continued investigation."

After he drove away, the family gathered again in the family room, the cookies now forgotten on their plate.

"What do we do next?" Ellie asked, voicing what they were all thinking.

"We keep looking," Mr. Finch said firmly.

"And maybe," Angie added, "we need to take a closer look at the Collins gallery. After all, they're right in the middle of the area where that call originated."

As they continued their discussion, none of them noticed Euclid and Circe sitting alert by the window, their attention fixed on the darkness outside.

13

It was early morning when Angie worked at the long counter. The kitchen was her safe place, a spot where creativity and comfort merged into delicious possibilities. Today she was developing new recipes for the bake shop, starting with an elegant dessert of strawberries with vanilla cream and puff pastry.

From their usual spot on top of the refrigerator, Euclid and Circe watched with keen interest as she combined mascarpone, heavy cream, fresh lemon zest, and a pinch of kosher salt in a large mixing bowl. The cats always seemed to know when something special was in the works.

Jenna sat at the kitchen island with her sketchbook open before her as she worked on new jewelry designs. She looked up as Angie began whipping the cream mixture to soft peaks. “That looks delicious. The lemon zest is a nice touch.”

Ellie appeared beside Jenna, peeking over her shoulder at the sketches. “Oooh, such pretty earrings. The way you've wrapped those crystals is so delicate.”

“I was going to make something like this for the Academy Awards gift bags if I got the job.” Jenna adjusted a piece of wire. “I was disappointed when I wasn’t chosen this year, but the organizer told me that I had a good shot at getting a contract for next year’s Oscars.”

“I really hope that happens,” Angie told her twin. “It would be so exciting.”

The back door opened, letting in a burst of warm spring air along with Courtney and Mr. Finch returning from their morning walk.

“What's cookin'?” Courtney asked, heading straight for the faucet to pour herself a glass of cold water. The kitchen already smelled heavenly from the puff pastry baking in the oven.

“Plenty,” Jenna replied, adding shading to her sketch. “Angie's concocting some new recipes to feature in the bake shop.”

Mr. Finch sidled up to watch Angie work, his eyes bright with anticipation. “I love it when you make something new. I can't wait to try it." He peered at the rows of small glass bowls lined up precisely on the counter. "Your presentation is always so artistic."

The kitchen felt especially cozy this morning, with everyone taking a rare day off from their businesses to enjoy a return trip to Brimfield - this time purely for pleasure rather than investigation.

"When are we leaving?" Ellie asked, straightening a stack of recipe cards.

"As soon as I'm done with this dessert and all of you have given me feedback," Angie replied, checking the oven timer. "Could someone take the puff pastry out? It should be perfectly golden by now."

"I'll get it." Courtney grabbed an oven mitt and carefully removed the tray, releasing a cloud of buttery steam as she set it on the counter to cool. "Wow, look at those layers."

Working efficiently, Angie began assembling the desserts. She spooned the vanilla cream into the glass bowls, creating perfect swirls that she alternated with layers of fresh strawberries, their red color vibrant against the white cream. Once the puff pastry had cooled slightly, she broke it into delicate shards and arranged them artfully on top. A sprinkle of finely chopped pistachios added the finishing touch.

"Okay," she announced, stepping back to survey her work. "It's ready. Come get a bowl."

The family members needed no second invitation. They gathered around, accepting their portions with eager anticipation. The first bites were met with appreciative silence, broken only by happy sighs.

"Well? What do you think?" Angie asked, though their expressions told her everything she needed to know.

"We can't say anything because we're concentrating on eating it," Courtney managed between spoonfuls. "This might be your best creation yet."

"It is absolutely sublime, Miss Angie," Mr. Finch declared, scraping his bowl clean. "A surefire winner with your customers. The contrast between the crisp pastry and creamy filling is perfect."

"Can I put out some for the B&B guests for the mid-morning snack?" Ellie asked hopefully. "They'll love this."

"That's a good idea. There's plenty left." Angie began preparing more portions while Courtney started packing a cooler with drinks and snacks for their Brimfield adventure.

Thirty minutes later, with the kitchen restored to

order and the B&B guests happily sampling their treats, the family piled into Ellie's van. Gigi and Libby bounced excitedly in their car seats, already asking if there would be ice cream at the market.

The spring morning had blossomed into a perfect day for outdoor shopping - warm sunshine, a light breeze, and clear blue skies. As they drove away from Sweet Cove, leaving their investigation concerns behind for a few hours, the van filled with sunny chatter about what treasures they might find at the market.

"Remember," Mr. Finch cautioned with a twinkle in his eye, "we're going just for fun today. No detective work allowed."

But as they all knew, in their world, you never knew when or where the next clue might appear - even on a simple family outing to a flea market.

The spring sunshine warmed the wide fields of the Brimfield Market, where hundreds of tents and canopies stretched as far as the eye could see. The air was filled with a festive mix of voices, music from various performers, and the occasional call of birds overhead. Delicious aromas wafted from food trucks offering everything from gourmet grilled cheese to authentic Thai cuisine.

The family had come prepared for a full day of treasure hunting. Their red wagon, cushioned with comfortable pillows, served as a perfect chariot for Gigi and Libby when their little legs grew tired of walking. For now, though, the girls skipped ahead excitedly, pointing out things to each other.

“Look at this gorgeous copper pot,” Ellie said, examining a gleaming vessel at an antiques booth. “It would be perfect for our kitchen.” After some good-natured haggling, she added it to the wagon.

Courtney found vintage art books for the gallery, while Jenna discovered unique precious stones she could use in her jewelry designs. Mr. Finch seemed content to simply observe, though his eyes lit up when he found a vendor selling hand-crafted canes and walking sticks.

“Ice cream time!” Angie announced when they reached a vendor selling homemade varieties. Soon everyone was enjoying colorful cones - chocolate chip for the girls, maple walnut for Mr. Finch, and various other flavors for the sisters.

“This is just what we needed.” Courtney sighed contentedly. “A day away from work, mysteries, and suspicious characters.”

In a few minutes, those words would prove to be ironic.

As Jenna and Angie stood, admiring delicately carved scrimshaw pieces at a nautical booth, Gigi suddenly tugged at her mother's sleeve.

"Momma," she said in a serious voice that seemed too old for her years. "See that man over there? I don't think he's very nice."

Angie's motherly instincts immediately went into overdrive. "Where, honey? Who do you mean?"

Gigi pointed across the crowded aisle to a booth near the end of the row. A young man in crisp chinos and a long-sleeved shirt stood talking intently with a vendor who had paintings and rare coins displayed.

Angie's heart skipped a beat as recognition dawned on her. From the photographs they'd looked at and the descriptions given by people who had seen him, the young man appeared to be a perfect match for Donald Prior.

Jenna stepped closer to her twin, their shoulders touching. "Is that...?"

"It sure seems so." Angie's voice was barely above a whisper. "Let's get closer."

They started down the aisle, pulling the wagon behind them, but the market had grown crowded as more shoppers arrived. They found themselves stuck behind a group examining a large piece of furniture, forced to wait as the transaction was completed. By the time they could move again, the young man had vanished.

When they reached the booth where he'd been standing, Jenna addressed the vendor. “You were just speaking with a young man a few minutes ago.”

The vendor, an older man with weathered hands, stared at her blankly.

“Do you know who he is? Do you know his name?” Jenna pressed.

“I don't know who he is.” The man shrugged. “I think he walked that way.” He gestured vaguely toward another row of booths.

“What did he want?” Angie asked the vendor.

The man’s face clouded. “He didn’t want anything ... not that it’s any of your business.”

Despite searching several aisles, they found no trace of the mysterious young man. The market's layout, with its maze of booths and shifting crowds, made it easy for someone to disappear quickly.

Angie knelt beside the wagon where both girls sat quietly watching. “Why do you think that man wasn't nice, honey?” She and the other family members knew both little girls had the ability to sense things even at their young age.

Gigi shrugged, her small face serious. "I could just tell."

Libby looked at her mom and her Aunt Angie. "I think he steals things," she added suddenly, her blue eyes wide.

"What do you mean, sweetheart?" Jenna asked her daughter gently.

Libby shook her head, clutching her stuffed bunny. "I don't know. He's bad."

Angie and Jenna exchanged meaningful looks. Like their mothers before them, the girls were developing their own intuitive abilities. Before they could question the children further, they spotted Ellie, Courtney, and Mr. Finch making their way through the crowd, arms full of purchases.

"There you are," Courtney called. "We found the most amazing vintage..." She stopped, noting their serious expressions. "What's wrong?"

They quickly shared what had happened.

Mr. Finch leaned on his cane with a thoughtful expression. "Interesting. What's that young man doing here, talking to a vendor selling paintings?"

"Nothing good." Courtney scowled, her earlier carefree mood evaporating. "Do you think he's trying to arrange a sale?"

"Or testing the waters to see if certain vendors

might be willing to handle stolen goods," Ellie suggested quietly.

The festive atmosphere of their family outing had shifted, the bright sunshine somehow less warm. Around them, other shoppers continued their treasure hunting, unaware of the possibility of darker currents flowing beneath the market's light-hearted surface.

"Should we call Chief Martin?" Jenna asked.

"And tell him what?" Angie sighed. "That we might have seen someone who might be Donald Prior talking to a vendor who claims not to know him? We need more than that to make it worth his while to drive out here."

"At least we know Donald Prior is in the area," Mr. Finch pointed out with a raised eyebrow, "and apparently interested in art dealers."

Gigi and Libby had gone quiet in their wagon, both girls watching the crowds with serious expressions. Their cups of ice cream, partially eaten, were forgotten in their hands.

"Perhaps we should head home," Ellie suggested.

But Angie shook her head. "No. We're not letting him spoil our family day. The girls were looking forward to the puppet show at the children's area, and I spotted a booth selling vintage cookie cutters I want to check out."

"Agreed," Mr. Finch said firmly. "We'll keep our eyes open, but we're here to enjoy ourselves. Though I think we should all stay together now."

They continued their market exploration, but each face in the crowd got a second look. The carefree morning had evolved into something more complicated - much like their investigation itself.

As they made their way toward the children's area, Angie felt that somewhere in this vast market, Donald Prior could be watching them too. What would he do with the knowledge that they were so close to finding him?

The puppet show's cheerful music drifted across the field, and the girls perked up at the sound. *Sometimes,* Angie thought, *the best thing to do is to simply keep moving forward, keeping one eye on the shadows while still walking in the light.*

14

The late morning sun created dappled shadows through the mature maple trees lining the exclusive neighborhood where Paul Benson, the man who was walking the path near the Harrington mansion on the night of the theft, and his family lived. The enormous Colonial-style home with white clapboard siding and black shutters sat back from the street. Purple and white irises bloomed in perfectly maintained beds, and a curved brick walkway led to a glossy black door with gleaming brass hardware.

Clustered rhododendrons provided privacy from neighboring houses while still allowing glimpses of the sea beyond the carefully landscaped back garden. The property spoke of success, taste, and attention to detail - perhaps too much attention, Angie thought as she noticed how precisely the hedges were trimmed.

As she and Chief Martin approached the house and rang the bell, the door opened almost immediately. Paul Benson stood there, his black Lab Max at his heel, both seeming tense despite the casual setting.

Paul wore expensive-looking khakis and a blue oxford shirt. A silver Rolex gleamed on his wrist - the kind of watch that spoke of wealth.

"Hello. Come in, please," he said, his hand nervously adjusting his collar. "We can talk in the living room."

The interior of the house matched its exterior in understated elegance, though Angie noticed subtle signs of recent redecoration - fresh paint, new furniture, artwork that still had that just-hung look. The living room featured built-in bookshelves filled with leather-bound medical texts and family photos, comfortable furniture in subtle earth tones, and large windows overlooking the manicured back garden. A baby grand piano occupied one corner, its surface decorated with framed photographs showing Benson's children's progression from toddlers to accomplished young adults.

"We appreciate you seeing us," Chief Martin said as they settled into the seating area. Max laid down at Paul's feet, but his friendly demeanor seemed subdued, matching his owner's mood. The dog's dark eyes moved between the visitors and his owner, as if sensing the underlying tension.

"Of course," Paul replied, his fingers drumming a quiet rhythm on his chair arm. "Though I'm not sure what else I can tell you about that night."

"Dad?" a young woman's voice called from somewhere in the house. "Are you talking to someone? Alan and I just got back from our run."

"Yes, sweetheart. The police chief and Ms. Roseland are here. Come say hello."

Footsteps approached, and two young people entered the room together. The Benson twins were striking - both tall and athletic, with their father's dark hair and their absent mother's fine bone structure evident in the family photos on the piano. Alice wore her hair in a sleek professional bob that framed her face perfectly, while Alan's was expertly styled in the casual-but-expensive way that suggested regular visits to an upscale salon. Both were dressed in coordinating running outfits that probably cost more than most people's entire workout wardrobes.

"Alice and Alan are home from college for a couple of weeks," Paul explained, obvious pride momentarily replacing his nervous energy. "They graduate from Princeton at the end of the month."

"With honors," Alan added, his smile confident. "I'm heading to Yale Law in the fall. I already have an apartment lined up in New Haven."

"And I'll be at Harvard Law," Alice chimed in, perching on the arm of the sofa. "But first, we both have summer internships lined up with law firms in Boston. I'll be with Blackwell & Stone, specializing in art and cultural property law."

"Harrison Law for me," Alan added quickly, as if not wanting his sister to dominate the conversation.

"Impressive credentials," Chief Martin noted, studying the twins. "You must know this neighborhood pretty well, having grown up here. Ever use that trail near the Harringtons' property?"

The twins exchanged a quick glance before Alice answered. "Sometimes, when we were younger we did. It's a nice walking path."

"Beautiful views of the ocean," Alan added. "Though we haven't been back there much since high school."

"Speaking of the trail," the chief turned to Paul,

"could you walk us through exactly what you saw that night? Your exact route?"

Paul shifted in his chair, his hand going to his collar again. "I usually take Max down Maple to Ocean Drive, then circle back using the cliff trail. That night..." He paused, as if carefully considering his words. "That night was no different."

"What time did you start your walk?"

"Around midnight, I think. Maybe a bit later. I'd had a long surgery that day..."

"Dad's schedule can be quite demanding," Alice interrupted. "He often walks late to decompress."

The chief made a note. "Did you see any vehicles parked along the trail access points? Or anywhere unusual?"

"I don't..." Paul started, but Alan cut in.

"Dad, didn't you mention seeing an unfamiliar van that night? Near the beach access?"

Paul's expression flickered with something that looked fleetingly like surprise or concern before smoothing out. "Yes, now that Alan mentions it, there was a dark-colored van. I didn't think much of it at the time."

"You didn't mention that in your first statement," Chief Martin observed mildly.

"Details keep coming back to me," Paul said, his

fingers now tapping rapidly on the chair arm. "At the time, it all seemed so unimportant. There was no need to pay close attention."

"Let's focus on the men you saw in the Harringtons' backyard," the chief pressed. "You said they were moving purposefully. Can you elaborate?"

"They seemed to know where they were going," Paul said, glancing briefly at his children. "Not like tourists who sometimes wander up there to look at the view. They moved ... efficiently. They were on the Harringtons' property so I thought they might be guests."

"How many men exactly?"

"Two, I think. Yes, definitely two. One was taller than the other."

"Could you hear them speaking? Any accents or distinctive voices?"

Paul's hand went to his watch, adjusting it unnecessarily. "No, they were too far away. But they seemed ... professional."

"Professional?" Angie asked, catching the odd choice of words.

"I mean... they moved like they had a purpose," Paul corrected quickly.

Alice stood suddenly, moving to the window.

"Dad has excellent observational skills. It's part of being a surgeon - you have to notice details."

"Very true," the chief agreed. "Which makes me wonder what other details you might have noticed that night, Dr. Benson. Any other vehicles? People walking dogs? Lights in houses?"

"No, nothing like that. It was a quiet night. Most people in this neighborhood go early to bed."

"Except the Harringtons don't always go to bed early," Alan added, then seemed to regret speaking when his sister shot him a sharp look.

"Did you know about Mr. Harrington's hearing impairment?" the chief asked casually.

Paul's fingers stopped their tapping. "Everyone in the neighborhood knew he was hard of hearing. I imagine he took his hearing aid out at night." He paused. "I suppose that made him vulnerable."

"As a doctor," the chief noted, "you must know a lot about sleep patterns and medications."

"I don't see how that's relevant," Alice said quickly, moving back to stand near her father's chair.

Max whined softly from his spot on the floor, and Paul reached down to scratch behind the dog's ears. His hand seemed to be trembling slightly.

"Have you noticed any other unusual activity in

the neighborhood lately?" Angie asked, trying to ease the growing tension.

"No, nothing at all," Paul said firmly. "In retrospect, I should have called the police right away when I saw those men in the Harringtons' backyard so late at night, but I didn't want to seem like a nosy neighbor who was overreacting."

"We understand," Angie told him. "It's a common reaction when something like this happens."

Paul took a deep breath and nodded. "I apologize, but I really should be getting ready for work. I have surgery scheduled in two hours."

As they prepared to leave, Angie noticed the stack of art books on the coffee table. The top one was titled "Impressionist Masters and Their Markets," and beneath it was a volume about art crime and recovery.

"Are you interested in art, Mr. Benson?" she asked.

"Those are mine," Alice said quickly, "for a paper I'm writing on art law and insurance validation. It's fascinating how many pieces go missing and are never recovered."

In the foyer, Max whined again as they said their goodbyes. The dog's dark eyes seemed troubled, matching the underlying mood in the elegant house. Through the doorway to the living room, Angie caught a glimpse of Alan placing a protective hand on his father's shoulder.

Outside, walking to the chief's car, Angie turned to him. "He remembered a lot more details this time."

"Yes, he did," the chief agreed, looking back at the house. "And did you notice how his children kept jumping in to explain things? Almost like they were trying to control the conversation."

"The art books seemed like a coincidence too," Angie mused. "As did Alice's interest in art law."

As they drove away from the Benson house, the perfectly maintained Colonial grew smaller in the rearview mirror, its polished windows reflecting the late morning sun like knowing eyes.

"There's something else," Angie said finally. "The way Dr. Benson described the thieves as being 'coordinated,' 'professional,' and 'efficient.' I don't think those are the words of someone who just caught a glimpse of some shadows in the dark."

"No," the chief agreed. "Those are the words of someone who had a much better view than he's admitting."

Angie nodded. "And the timing of that dog walk was too convenient."

They stopped at a traffic light, and the chief turned to look at her. "We need to look more into the Benson family, their finances, their connections, any trips they've taken recently, and especially any contact they might have had with the Collins gallery."

"Maybe the Benson family's interest in art is more than appreciation of technique and history .... maybe it extends to stealing art," Angie speculated.

As they pulled up to the Victorian, Angie asked, "Chief, what if the art books aren't just for Alice's paper? What if they're research? Learning about how stolen art moves through the black market?"

"And how to avoid the legal pitfalls," the chief finished, "which is exactly what you'd want to know if you were planning something like this."

They sat in silence for a moment, watching the spring breeze ruffle the flower petals in the Victorian's garden. The mystery of the Harrington theft may have just taken another turn. As Angie climbed out of the car, she felt certain they were finally starting to uncover the truth - even if that truth involved one of the most respected neighbors in Silver Cove.

"We'll keep an eye on them," the chief said before she closed the car door. "Be careful. If they are involved, they've got a lot to lose."

Angie nodded, watching the police car pull away. Inside the Victorian, she knew her sisters would be eager to hear about the interview, but first, she needed to think over what they'd learned about the perfect family in their perfect house, who might be hiding some very imperfect secrets.

15

A cool breeze carried the scent of late spring roses across the manicured lawn of Lara Harrington Stone's Silver Cove estate. Like her parents' home, the large Colonial was impressive, though it lacked the warmth and character of the Harrington mansion. Everything here felt more structured, from the perfectly symmetrical landscaping to the gleaming brass door knocker.

Lara herself matched her home's formal appearance. In her fifties, she carried herself with an air of someone accustomed to commanding hospital rooms. Her steel-gray hair was styled in an expensive cut that probably required weekly maintenance, and her clothes - though casual for a weekend morning -

were clearly designer. *Not a thread out of place*, Angie thought, *just like everything around her*.

"Thank you for seeing us," Courtney said as they settled into the sunroom. The space was immaculate but somehow sterile, lacking the lived-in comfort of her parents' home. Family photos on the walls showed Lara and her husband - both successful doctors - with their two sons, now in their thirties. One lived in Los Angeles, and the other in Boston, according to Chief Martin's notes.

"I was shocked to hear about the art heist," Lara told them, her posture rigid in her chair. "Thank heavens my father didn't wake up when the thieves were there, and thankfully, my mother wasn't at home when they broke into the house. I've been warning them for years to get the security system updated," she continued, a note of frustration creeping into her controlled voice, "but they always put it off. My parents are too trusting. They're almost gullible." The way she said the last word carried a hint of long-standing irritation.

Lara poured tea from a silver service, her movements precise and practiced - everything measured and proper.

"The police think that someone who visited

during the holiday house tour might have been casing the property," Angie said carefully, watching Lara's reaction. "They believe one of the visitors may have been involved in planning the heist."

Lara's hand flew to her mouth, her perfect composure cracking slightly. "My parents are very generous with their time and money. Too generous, if you ask me. I always tell them not to get involved with things like the holiday tour. Letting strangers into their home isn't a safe thing to do. And here's the result." She let out a long slow breath as she shook her head, her diamond tennis bracelet catching the light.

"Are you close to your parents?" Courtney asked, accepting a cup of tea.

Lara looked surprised by the question, her eyes narrowing slightly. "Of course, I am. Why would you ask such a thing? It seems an inappropriate question." Her fingers tightened around her teacup.

"I'm asking because if you see each other frequently, you might have noticed things," Courtney explained smoothly. "Maybe someone came to their door asking for donations, or they received odd phone calls. Perhaps hospital staff asked strange questions about your mother's upcoming surgery and her home situation. If you talk often, they might have mentioned something small but unusual."

"I see." Lara relaxed a little, though her guard remained firmly in place.

"Do you see your parents often?" Angie pressed gently.

"We talk frequently, but neither of them mentioned anything odd." She stood and walked to the window, looking out over her immaculate garden. "Though they probably wouldn't have noticed if something was odd. As I said, they're rather naive about such things."

Angie noticed how Lara's reflection in the window showed a fleeting expression of what might have been concern - or maybe, guilt. "Were you involved in the holiday tour preparations at your parents' house?"

"Certainly not," Lara replied quickly. "I told Mother it was a terrible idea. All those strangers tramping through the house, examining everything." She turned back to face them. "The art collection alone was reason enough to refuse, but Mother insisted it was 'good for the community.'" Her tone made it clear what she thought of that reasoning. "At least they removed some of the paintings from the walls prior to the event."

"Were you there during the tour?" Courtney pressed.

"Briefly. I had hospital rounds that day." Lara's hand went to her bracelet. "I stopped by my parents' house to make sure everything was going okay."

"Did you notice anyone paying particular attention to the layout of the house? Or asking questions about security?"

"No, but then, I wasn't really focused on the visitors." She paused, then added, "Though there was one young man - a volunteer, I believe - who seemed very knowledgeable about art. Mother was quite impressed with him."

Angie and Courtney exchanged glances. "Do you remember his name?"

"Donald something. He was supposedly a graduate student." Lara's lips thinned. "Another example of my parents being too trusting. They'll talk to anyone who shows interest in them."

As if on cue, a phone buzzed somewhere in the room. "Excuse me," Lara said, "but I have patients to check on. Was there anything else?"

Angie and Courtney thanked her for her time

and made their goodbyes, both noting how quickly she ushered them toward the door. Outside, the spring morning had grown warmer, but something about Lara Harrington Stone's perfect house left them feeling chilly.

"Well," Courtney said as they walked to their car, "that was interesting."

"Very," Angie agreed. "Did you notice how defensive she got about her relationship with her parents? And that comment about them being 'naive?'"

"Almost like she resents them," Courtney mused, "or resents something about them."

They drove away from the estate, both thinking about the daughter who lived so close to her parents but seemed emotionally distant. Another piece of the puzzle, perhaps, but did it fit with what they already knew about the theft?

"We should tell the chief about her reaction to Donald," Angie said finally, "and maybe look into her financial situation. Being a doctor pays well, but maintaining this lifestyle is expensive."

Courtney nodded, understanding what her sister wasn't saying. Sometimes the people closest to us could be the ones we least suspect - or the ones we should suspect first.

The difference between the sisters couldn't have been more striking. Where Lara's Colonial mansion had been all manicured perfection, Brenda Harrington Hills' farmhouse welcomed visitors with cheerful chaos. The white clapboard home needed painting in spots, but climbing roses and wisteria softened its weathered charm. Two friendly golden retrievers bounded across the yard to greet Angie and Courtney, while a tabby cat watched regally from its place on the porch railing.

"Welcome!" Brenda called from the garden, where she'd been picking flowers. Her curly gray-blonde hair escaped from a casual braid, and her paint-splattered denim shirt suggested a morning spent on her art. "Come in, come in! Don't mind the dogs - they think everyone's here to see them."

Inside, sunlight streamed through windows and warm light revealed a home full of life and creativity. Grandchildren's artwork covered the refrigerator, handmade pottery filled open shelves, and musical instruments waited in corners for the next impromptu concert.

"Let me show you around while the lemonade chills," Brenda offered, leading them through the rambling house. Through the back windows, they could see a couple of horses grazing in a field. "Our five kids are all grown now, but they love coming home with their kids. There's always room for everyone here. Come out to the studio. I'll bring the lemonade with us."

Brenda's studio occupied what had once been a barn, converted with lots of windows to capture the natural light. A large floor loom dominated one corner, its half-finished weaving showing rich earth tones. A pottery wheel sat near French doors that opened onto a wildflower meadow, and easels displayed several mixed-media paintings alive with color and movement.

"Please, sit," Brenda said, gesturing to comfortable chairs arranged near a window overlooking her garden. The chairs, though mismatched, invited relaxation in a way her sister's formal furniture never could. She poured lemonade into hand-thrown pottery cups, the drink garnished with fresh mint from her garden.

"We spoke yesterday with your sister," Angie said, accepting her cup.

Brenda's warm smile held a touch of sadness. "We're sisters but about as opposite as two people can be. Lara likes to be in control of everything. I always tell her she might be happier if she loosened up a little." She chuckled. "She never appreciates my suggestions."

"Do you get along?" Courtney asked, noticing how one of the dogs had settled at Brenda's feet, while the other watched the meadow through the French doors.

"I love my sister. Are we close friends? Not really, not anymore. We're just too different. Lara used to be fun and relaxed, but she got so caught up in the life-style of her and her husband being two successful, wealthy doctors. She changed, and it makes me sad." Brenda adjusted her paint-smudged shirt absently. "Lara thinks I've squandered my life. I should have been a doctor like her. My husband Justin is a teacher, and we don't make enough money according to Lara. We live like hippies, she tells me." Her laugh was genuine and without bitterness. "My husband and I are very happy, our kids are happy, and that's what's important."

One of her cats wandered in, jumping onto a windowsill to watch a butterfly dancing past. The peaceful scene seemed worlds away from Lara's sterile sunroom.

"Did your parents mention anything unusual recently?" Courtney asked. "Anyone asking questions about the house, their schedules, your mother's surgery?"

"No, nothing like that. Mom was concerned about her surgery, but that's normal." Brenda's face softened with obvious affection. "I check in on them every day. We have coffee, take walks, or just sit and chat. We're close. They're good people."

"Your mother mentioned a young man who volunteered during the holiday tour," Angie said carefully.

"Yes, she told me about him. He knew so much about art, and they had a wonderful conversation." Suddenly, Brenda's expression turned worried. "You don't think he had anything to do with the heist, do you?"

"The police are looking into it," Angie explained gently.

"Oh, no." Brenda rubbed the back of her neck. "He may have been taking advantage of my mother? That's terrible."

A breeze stirred the wildflowers outside as Courtney asked, "Do you know of anyone who might have resented your parents? Had arguments with them?"

A slight smile played on Brenda's face. "My sister?"

"Does she resent them?"

"I'd say she does. She never agrees with what they do." Brenda looked thoughtful and slightly sad, her fingers tracing the rim of her lemonade cup. "Just between us, my sister's husband Roland is a gambler. He's caused a lot of money problems for them. Lara asked our parents for a loan about five years ago, but they declined to give her what she wanted. She asked for a very large sum. They gave her half. She was livid and swore she would never forgive them."

"Did she soften her stance over time?" Angie asked, thinking of Lara's controlled demeanor.

"She didn't, and it got worse when my parents announced their estate plans." Brenda looked out at her peaceful property. "Lara resents that they're giving their fortune to charities. They paid for our children's educations, but they aren't giving anything else to family members. They believe inheriting large amounts of money can be detrimental. They say they gave us the skills and education necessary to be contributing members of society and that we should forge our own ways."

"How do you feel about that?" Courtney asked softly.

"I think they're right. It's their money. They'll be

doing communities a lot of good by leaving it to charities." She turned back to them, her face serene. "Besides, look at all this." She gestured to her studio, the meadow, and the distant horses. "What more could anyone need or want?"

"I have one last question," Angie told the woman. "Do you think your sister could steal from your parents?"

"No, absolutely not." Brenda shook her head. "No matter how resentful Lara feels toward them, I know for sure she would never do that."

As they prepared to leave, Brenda pressed jars of honey from her beehives into their hands. "From our bees," she said proudly. "They love the wildflowers."

Walking back to their car, they passed Brenda's husband returning from the local high school where he taught. He waved pleasantly, his car dusty from the country roads but his smile warm and genuine.

"Two sisters," Courtney mused as they drove away. "One has everything money can buy but wants more. The other has less money but seems to have everything that matters."

"And one of them," Angie added quietly, "has a desperate husband with gambling debts and a grudge against her parents."

They drove back toward Sweet Cove with the scent of wildflowers and honey lingering in the car.

Behind them, Brenda's windchimes tinkled in the breeze, a peaceful sound that somehow made the darker implications of what they'd learned even more concerning.

16

The moonlight peeked through the windows of Jenna's jewelry studio at the back of the Victorian, where the sisters had gathered for one of their regular jewelry-

assembling sessions to help Jenna get the work done. The warm light caught the sparkle of crystals and the gleam of silver wire as they worked on Jenna's latest designs. Soft music played in the background, and the sweet scent of spring flowers from Ellie's garden drifted in through the slightly open window.

Euclid and Circe had claimed opposite ends of the studio's comfortable sofa, where they were peacefully napping. Occasionally, one or the other would open an eye to check on their humans' progress, then return to their contented dozing.

"These new designs are beautiful, Jenna," Courtney said, holding up a pair of earrings that captured the light of the lamp. "The way you've wrapped the crystals makes them look like they're floating."

"I was inspired by dewdrops on spider webs," Jenna explained, demonstrating the wire-wrapping technique to Angie. "See how the silver cradles the stone but doesn't overwhelm it?"

Ellie, sorting crystals by color, looked up with a smile. "Your orders must be increasing with designs like these."

"They are," Jenna agreed. "Though honestly, it's hard to focus on jewelry with everything else going on. I keep thinking about all our suspects and their possible motives."

"Let's take a break," Angie suggested, setting down her pliers. "I made lemon bars earlier." She retrieved the treats and the teapot from the kitchen, and Ellie poured the hot tea into their favorite mugs.

"Okay," Courtney said, settling into a comfortable chair. "Let's sort through what we know. First, there's this Donald character who volunteered at the holiday tour last December."

"He can't be local," Jenna mused, curling up on the window seat. "Someone would have recognized him by now. Silver Cove isn't that big."

"Which means someone had to tell him about the Harringtons and their art collection," Ellie added. "He didn't just stumble onto this opportunity."

Angie nodded, passing around the lemon bars. "So, who's pulling his strings and how do we find them?"

"And how many other holiday home tours has he cased?" Courtney wondered. "He seemed to know exactly what he was doing."

They fell silent for a moment, considering.

"Then there's Dr. Benson and his perfectly polished twins," Ellie said finally. "They certainly had means and opportunity."

"But what's their motive?" Jenna asked. "Did they want the artwork for themselves? That seems risky for a respected doctor and his law-school-bound children."

"Unless they're not as financially secure as they appear," Courtney suggested. "Those Ivy League educations don't come cheap."

Angie sipped her tea thoughtfully. "Let's not

forget Lara and her gambling husband. That's a clear motive right there."

"Especially since they had to ask her parents for a loan," Ellie reminded them, "and Lara's obviously bitter about their inheritance plans."

Jenna said softly, "A gambling addiction can drive someone to extremes."

Circe stretched on the sofa and then moved to Angie's lap.

"What about the Collins gallery owners?" Courtney asked. "Something was definitely off there. Beth seemed almost afraid of Nathan at times."

"They weren't exactly forthcoming with information," Ellie agreed. "Plus, that strange phone call to Mrs. Harrington originated near Brimfield, right where their gallery is located."

"Too many suspects." Angie sighed, stroking Circe's fur. "Too many possible motives."

"We still don't know what's special about that Renoir," Jenna added. "Why did the caller specifically mention details about it?"

The studio door opened then, and Mr. Finch appeared. "Good evening, my dears. Working on the lovely jewelry, I see."

"Join us, Mr. Finch," Ellie invited, reaching for

another mug. "We're taking a break with tea and lemon bars."

He settled into his favorite chair, accepting the offered refreshments. "Quite a gathering of talent in this room," he observed, looking around at their work. "Creative souls, all of you."

Something in his tone made Angie look at him more closely. "Have you been working on something new yourself, Mr. Finch?"

"Indeed, I have, Miss Angie. Would you care to see it?"

Angie's sisters looked at one another, all noticing the slight tension that had crept into their sister's posture. Even Euclid lifted his head from his nap, watching the exchange with interest.

After taking a deep breath, Angie said with reluctance, "I think I'd better take a look."

The words hung in the air like the last notes of a song, and somehow, they all knew that whatever Mr. Finch had to show Angie could change the course of their investigation.

The evening had deepened into twilight as the sisters and their feline companions followed Mr.

Finch to his apartment off the Victorian's family room. The space had been thoughtfully designed when they'd added it for their adopted family member after he sold his house to their friends, the Abels. Originally, Mr. Finch had lived in the mansion with the family, but having his own apartment gave him independence while keeping him close.

His apartment was a perfect reflection of the man himself - warm, elegant, and filled with artistic touches. The combination living/dining room opened to a well-equipped kitchen, where he often baked treats for Gigi and Libby. One and a half bathrooms and a large bedroom provided all the comfort he needed, but his favorite room - and the heart of his creative life - was the spacious sunroom.

Now, in the gathering darkness, that sunroom held something that made Angie's stomach tighten with anticipation. She knew what looking at Mr. Finch's paintings could do to her - the trances she fell into often left her exhausted and fighting migraines but also often provided crucial clues to their investigations.

"Are you ready to see the painting?" Mr. Finch asked gently, knowing what he was asking of her.

Angie managed a small smile. "No, but I'll look at it anyway."

"Come into the sunroom," Mr. Finch invited, leading the way into the spacious room where moonlight now streamed through the windows. An easel stood in the center with a white sheet draped carefully over the canvas.

Jenna, ever practical, carried over a comfortable chair and positioned it carefully in front of the easel. "Here, Angie. You'll need to sit for this."

Euclid and Circe sat on either side of Angie's chair like faithful guardians, while her sisters settled onto the nearby sofa. It was as if the room held its breath as Angie closed her eyes.

"Just give me a minute to prepare myself." She took several deep breaths, trying to clear her mind of their earlier discussions about suspects and motives. The familiar scent of oil paints and the smell of Mr. Finch's earlier baking centered her.

When she finally opened her eyes, she nodded. "I'm ready."

Mr. Finch carefully removed the sheet, revealing a painting of a mansion at night. The windows glowed warmly against the darkness, and a nearly full moon cast silver light over the grounds. The brushwork was masterful, creating an atmosphere both beautiful and somehow ominous.

As Angie stared at the canvas, the familiar sensation began. The room around her faded as she was drawn into the painting, the physical world dissolving into a vision.

The mansion's defined lines began to pulse, fading and then becoming bolder. The windows blazed with an intensity that made her eyes water, their glow seeming to reach out of the canvas. From the tree line, a figure emerged, dressed in black and wrapped in shadows. Try as she might, Angie couldn't make out the face, but something about the figure's movement seemed hauntingly familiar.

The dark figure approached the house with practiced stealth. Suddenly, the sharp sound of breaking glass shattered the night's silence. Voices drifted through the vision, but Angie could still only see the one figure clearly.

Then something extraordinary happened. A painting in a golden frame seemed to float out through the broken door, rising slowly into the night sky. Angie watched, mesmerized, as the breeze carried it up and over the trees until it disappeared into the darkness.

The vision shifted abruptly. Now she stood

outside a large brick building. A gunshot cracked through the night, followed by a heart-wrenching scream. Angie turned toward the sound and saw a figure crumpled on the ground, blood streaming from wounds that gleamed black in the moonlight. Though she couldn't see the person's face, a terrible certainty gripped her - this was someone they knew.

With a gasp that seemed to tear her from the vision, Angie's eyes flew open. She swayed in the chair, nearly falling, but Mr. Finch's steady hands caught her shoulders.

"Easy now," he murmured, as Jenna hurried over with a glass of cool water.

Angie's hands shook as she sipped, her head already beginning to pound. The cats pressed against her legs, offering comfort by being near her.

"Did you see anything?" Courtney asked softly, knowing how fragile these moments could be.

They helped Angie to the sofa, where she rested her head back, gathering her thoughts. The vision was already starting to fade like a dream, but certain images remained sharp and terrifying.

"Someone was shot," she said finally, her voice barely above a whisper. "I couldn't see who it was, but..." She swallowed hard. "I had the feeling we knew them. Know them."

Her sisters shared worried glances as they gently questioned her about other details. Angie answered as best she could, though each word seemed to increase the pounding in her head.

"The painting - it floated away like it was being carried by the wind. And there was just one figure, but I heard another voice." She pressed her fingers to her temples. "I'm exhausted. I could fall asleep right here."

"Let the vision settle for a day or two," Mr. Finch suggested, drawing a light blanket over her shoulders. "You may learn more if you simply let your mind work on it subconsciously."

Ellie helped Angie stand, supporting her sister as they made their way to the kitchen. Mr. Finch heated milk for everyone, adding a touch of honey and cinnamon - his special remedy for troubled nights.

As they sipped their warm milk in the comfort of the familiar kitchen, none of them spoke about the violence in Angie's vision, but they all felt it - the sense that their investigation was about to take a dark turn.

"Time for bed," Jenna said finally, noting how Angie's eyes were struggling to stay open.

They said their goodnights to Mr. Finch and

made their way back into the main house, and Euclid and Circe followed close behind.

As Angie crawled into bed beside her husband, the last thing she saw before sleep claimed her was the image of that floating painting, the golden frame gleaming in the moonlight and carrying its secrets into the darkness. Somewhere in that vision lay the key to solving their mystery - if only they could understand it in time to prevent the violence she'd foreseen.

17

It was late afternoon when Mr. Finch and Courtney sat at the Victorian's kitchen island surrounded by planning calendars and course catalogs. Euclid and Circe watched with interest from atop the refrigerator as the two gallery owners discussed expanding their community programs.

"What about watercolor classes for beginners?" Courtney suggested, making notes in her leather-bound planner. "Sarah Jensen mentioned she'd be interested in teaching, and she has such a gentle way with nervous students."

"Excellent idea, my dear." Mr. Finch adjusted his reading glasses as he reviewed their list. "And perhaps we could add that pottery workshop you mentioned. The summer tourists would enjoy creating their own seaside memories."

"We'd need to invest in a few wheels and a kiln," Courtney mused, "but the basement space would be perfect for a studio." She paused, tapping her pen thoughtfully. "What about your sketching classes, Mr. Finch? Your students always rave about them."

The older man's eyes twinkled. "I suppose I could offer another session. Though, perhaps, we should wait until this current investigation we're working on is complete."

Their discussion was interrupted by the sound of the bakery door closing and Angie's tired footsteps approaching. Both looked up as she entered the kitchen, immediately noting her drawn expression.

"Hey, sis. What's cookin'?" Courtney set down her pen, concerned. "You look tired."

"I am tired," Angie admitted, moving to the sink for a glass of water. The kitchen still held the lingering warmth and sweet aromas from the day's baking - vanilla, cinnamon, and the fresh strawberries she'd used in her morning scones. "I couldn't sleep at all last night. That vision kept swirling in my brain like autumn leaves in a storm."

"Why don't we take a break from planning, Miss

Courtney?" Mr. Finch suggested, gathering their papers.

"What were you working on?" Angie asked, leaning against the counter and trying to focus on normal conversation.

"Planning summer and fall classes for the gallery," Courtney explained. "We're thinking of expanding our offerings - watercolors, pottery, and maybe even some art history lectures. Though right now..." She studied her sister's face carefully, "I'm more interested in what's keeping you awake."

"Did anything come to mind while your brain was working on the puzzle?" Mr. Finch asked, his expression gentle but keen.

Angie sipped her water slowly, gathering her thoughts. Outside, a goldfinch landed on the bird feeder, its bright yellow feathers catching the late afternoon light. The simple beauty of the moment contrasted sharply with her inner turmoil.

"Want to take a drive with me?" she asked finally.

"As long as it leads to adventure." Courtney's eyes lit up with interest as she began gathering her materials. "Where do you want to go?"

"To the Collins International Art Gallery."

"Can we ask why?" Courtney was already sliding her notebook and laptop into her briefcase, her earlier planning session forgotten at the prospect of new developments.

"The brick building in my hallucination..." Angie paused, searching for the right words. "It reminded me of the gallery's location. My thoughts keep returning to our conversation with the gallery owners. I need to go there, but I don't know why."

Courtney looked over at Mr. Finch. "Ready for a possible adventure?"

"Always." The older man's eyes twinkled as he reached for his cane. "Though, perhaps, we should let your sisters know where we're going?"

"I'll text them," Courtney said, already typing on her phone. "Ellie's with the B&B guests, and Jenna has a jewelry client coming in soon."

The drive to the gallery wound through the Massachusetts countryside, and the sun shining through the trees cast dappled shadows across the road. They passed fields where early summer wildflowers nodded in the breeze.

It wasn't long before the converted mill building rose before them, its red brick walls glowing in the late afternoon light. The river behind the mill provided a constant sound of rushing water, though today it seemed more ominous than peaceful.

"Is it open?" Mr. Finch asked as they approached the entrance, his arm linked with Courtney's. "The light facing the sign is out."

"I see someone inside," Courtney reported, looking through the gleaming windows. "Just one person moving around."

Angie tried the door and was surprised when it opened easily. The gallery's usual pristine atmosphere felt different somehow - less polished and more unsettled. Their footsteps echoed on the hardwood floors as they entered, the sound seeming to bounce off walls that normally absorbed the sound with their elegant hangings.

The space felt wrong - shadows gathered in corners where track lighting normally illuminated masterpieces, and there was a stillness that felt more abandoned than peaceful. Even the air seemed different, stale rather than the carefully climate-controlled atmosphere that protected valuable artworks.

They heard movement from the other gallery room, and Beth Collins appeared, looking markedly different from their previous visit. Gone were the designer clothes and perfect styling, replaced by jeans and a simple sweater. Her face showed signs of strain, and her usual confident posture seemed diminished.

"We're closed today," she said automatically, then recognition flickered across her face. "Oh, hello. I'm sorry. We're not open today."

"Do you have a few minutes to chat?" Courtney asked, her voice gentle but firm.

Beth seemed about to refuse, her hand fidgeting with her sweater sleeve, but then something in her expression shifted. "I have a few minutes. What can I help you with?"

Mr. Finch stepped forward, his cane tapping softly on the hardwood floor. "As you know, we're researching the heist from the Harringtons' home in Silver Cove."

"Yes, I recall." Beth's voice was tight and controlled, but her fingers wouldn't stop moving - adjusting her sleeve, touching her neck, or smoothing her hair.

"Do you know a young man named Donald Prior?" Mr. Finch's question hung in the air between them.

"Donald? Prior? I don't think I know anyone named Donald." But something flickered in Beth's eyes before she could mask it.

Angie pulled out her phone, bringing up the photograph. "Here's a photo of him. You can't see the face very well." She watched carefully as she handed the phone to Beth.

For just an instant, Beth's eyes narrowed, and then she thrust the phone back at Angie. Her hand trembled slightly, though she tried to hide it by crossing her arms.

"I don't recognize him. Is he involved in the heist?"

"He might be a person of interest," Courtney said diplomatically. "The police would like to talk to him."

"I can't help you." Beth's voice was firm but brittle, like thin ice over deep water.

"Where's Nathan?" Angie asked, noting how Beth's shoulders tensed at the mention of her husband. "Is he out back? Maybe he could take a look at the photo."

"He's not here," Beth snapped, then visibly tried to soften her tone. "He's not working this week."

Through the gallery's windows, clouds passed over the sun, casting shifting shadows across the valuable artwork inside. The space seemed to grow smaller and more confining.

"Is he traveling to buy artwork?" Courtney asked,

wandering casually around the room and studying the paintings that looked different in the dimmed lighting.

"Something like that." Beth glanced anxiously out the window as her jaw muscles visibly tightened. The rushing of the river outside seemed louder in the tense silence.

The conversation played out with more questions asked and deflected, and other answers given that revealed nothing.

"Why is the gallery closed today?" Mr. Finch asked.

"I'm doing inventory and paperwork. I got behind when we were in Europe."

"Will you be back to regular hours tomorrow?" Courtney walked nonchalantly around the room, looking at the paintings.

"Probably."

Angie looked closely at Beth's face. "Is anything wrong?" she asked gently.

"Nothing's wrong. I'm just tired."

Angie noticed that the woman's lower lip trembled for a second.

"Have you heard anything that might have to do with the art theft? Anything at all could help."

Beth shook her head. "No, nothing at all. I've been very busy since we got back from our trip."

"Well, we don't want to take any more of your time." Mr. Finch stepped forward and offered his hand.

Beth shook with the older man and when she did, an electrical zap darted through Mr. Finch's fingers.

"Thank you for your time."

Outside in the parking lot, the sun was sinking behind the brick building.

"Did you feel something when you shook hands with her?" Angie asked once they were safely away from the gallery.

"I did." Mr. Finch's expression was troubled as he leaned on his cane. "Ms. Collins is in distress. I sense it involves her husband, Nathan, but there's more to it than marital difficulties."

"Did you pick up on what else might be troubling her?" Courtney asked, her gallery owner's instincts alert to the undercurrents they'd witnessed.

"Indeed." Mr. Finch looked back at the brick building, its windows now seeming more like worried eyes. "I believe it has something to do with the Harringtons' stolen paintings."

They stood in silence for a moment, the man's

words settling over them. A pair of crows called from nearby trees, their harsh cries seeming to underscore the uneasy feeling that had settled over them.

Something was very wrong at the Collins International Art Gallery - something that went beyond a simple closed day for inventory. Beth Collins was afraid, her husband was mysteriously absent, and somehow it seemed connected to their investigation.

What would they find when they pulled on this particular thread? And would they be ready for whatever unraveled?

18

The harbor waters sparkled as the Roseland family supervised final preparations aboard Josh's yacht. The yacht, normally used for business events, weddings, and private charters was being transformed into a floating wonderland for the hospital fundraiser. Crew members strung thousands of tiny white lights along the rails while florists arranged elegant centerpieces of white roses and blue hydrangeas.

"The tables look perfect," Ellie said. She was already dressed for the evening in a classic black column dress, their mother's cabochon necklace gleaming at her throat. "Though I'm worried about the weather forecast mentioning possible wind."

"The captain says we'll be fine," Josh assured her,

looking handsome in his tuxedo as he reviewed details with the catering staff. "We're well-protected in this part of the harbor."

Angie emerged from below deck, her midnight blue silk gown catching the light. "The dessert station is all set up." She looked at Rufus. "Nobody is around to see you do what you do. Would you mind?"

Courtney's husband grinned, clearly enjoying his role. With subtle gestures, he used the flames shooting from his fingertips to light the hundreds of candles placed strategically around the yacht's decks. His fire power made quick work of what would have taken staff an hour to complete.

"Show off," Courtney teased her husband affectionately, smoothing her deep purple gown. She turned to her sisters. "Remember last year when we tried to do this with regular lighters?"

The family members laughed.

As the sun descended beneath the horizon, the harbor reflected shades of gold, violet, and pink as guests began to arrive. Josh had arranged for valet parking at the dock, where uniformed attendants directed arrivals to the illuminated gangway. Security was unobtrusive but thorough - a necessity given the wealthy and important crowd that was expected.

Mr. Finch arrived early with Betty Hayes on his arm, both beaming. Betty's hair was perfectly styled, and her red dress looked striking against Mr. Finch's traditional tuxedo.

"The yacht looks magnificent," she said, accepting a glass of champagne. "Though I have to admit, I'm still getting my sea legs."

They were followed by Mel and Orla Abel, then Chief Martin and his wife Lucille. The chief looked almost transformed in his tuxedo, while Lucille wore a flattering navy gown that sparkled with tiny beads.

"The whole town's talking about this event," Lucille told Angie. "You've outdone yourselves as hosts."

More guests arrived steadily - hospital board members, local politicians, and prominent business owners. Lincoln and Rose Harrington made their entrance with Rose moving carefully but confidently despite her recent surgery. Her deep blue silk gown complemented Lincoln's classic tuxedo, and they moved together with the ease of a long-married couple.

Dr. Paul Benson and his wife Lesley arrived next, with their twins Alice and Alan trailing behind. Angie noticed how Alan seemed distracted, constantly checking his phone, while Alice looked elegant but somehow ill at ease in her pale pink gown. There was a tension between the siblings that hadn't been there in previous encounters.

The band, positioned perfectly to take advantage of the yacht's acoustics, struck up a lively tune as the deck filled with guests. The early evening air was perfect - warm with just enough breeze to carry the salt scent of the harbor.

"Everything's perfect," Josh murmured to Angie as they shared a quick dance. His hand was warm against her back as they moved across the deck. "The hospital CEO just told me we've already exceeded our fundraising goal."

"Thanks to your corporate sponsors." Angie smiled up at him. "Though I think my dessert table helped sell a few tickets."

The evening flowed smoothly through the necessary speeches - thankfully brief thanks to Ellie's careful planning. Appetizers circulated continuously with tiny crab cakes, mushroom tartlets, and other delicacies from Sweet Cove's finest caterers.

Jenna and Tom took a turn on the dance floor, while Courtney and Rufus chatted with hospital staff near the rail.

During a break between dances, Angie and Jenna found themselves near Paul Benson at the bar.

He told them he was already on his third scotch. His usual professional demeanor seemed slightly frayed.

"Lovely evening," Jenna said casually. "Almost as nice as that night of the heist when you were walking Max."

Paul's hand tightened on his glass, knuckles whitening. "Yes, well... it's been perfect weather for walking lately."

"Have you remembered anything else about that night?" Angie asked gently.

"No, nothing." His voice was firm, but his eyes wouldn't meet theirs. A drop of scotch spilled as he set his glass down too quickly. "If you'll excuse me, I should find my wife."

Later, Angie and Courtney joined the Harringtons, their daughters, and their sons-in-law at their table. Brenda Harrington Hills introduced her husband Justin and Lara's husband Roland Stone to the sisters. They all shook hands. Angie couldn't help but notice how Roland seemed bored and disinterested.

Lincoln said to his sons-in-law, "These are some of the young women who are working with the police to investigate the heist."

While Justin smiled and thanked the sisters for volunteering with law enforcement, Roland barely made eye contact, and a few moments later, he stood and headed for the bar without saying a word.

Angie turned to Rose and asked how she was doing.

“My knee is doing well,” she told the sisters, patting Lincoln's hand. “And we're trying to focus on our blessings. We have each other, our health, and our wonderful community.”

“The whole town supports you,” Courtney assured them. “Everyone wants those paintings returned.”

Sadness flickered in Rose’s eyes, and Lincoln's face darkened slightly when he said, “We have to accept the fact that our art pieces might never come back. But Rose is right - we have much to be thankful for.”

Across the deck, Angie noticed Alan Benson in what appeared to be an intense conversation with Roland Stone and a man she didn't recognize. His sister, Alice, watched from a distance, worry evident in her expression.

The dessert buffet was being set up by Angie’s employees under her direction when Alice approached her. The young woman seemed to gather her courage before speaking.

“Angie? Could I speak with you?”

After excusing herself, Angie turned to give Alice her full attention. They made polite small talk about law school plans and summer internships before Alice's expression grew serious.

"I've noticed something odd recently," she said, twirling her champagne glass nervously. The lights reflected off the crystals on her dress, creating dancing patterns on the pale pink gown.

"Have you?" Angie kept her voice neutral but encouraging.

"My brother has been distant lately."

"About something specific or in general?"

Alice's eyes drifted to where Alan stood with his mysterious companions. "We used to be very close, but he seems to be pulling away from me. We used to tell each other everything, but now..." She trailed off, biting her lip.

"Have you talked to him about it?"

"No, I haven't. I don't want to accuse him of being less close with me." She sighed, the sound almost lost in the music. "He seems to have a couple of new friends and spends a lot of time with them. I don't even know their names."

"What about your parents? Do they think Alan is being distant or secretive with them?"

"I haven't brought it up." Alice swallowed hard,

looking young and sad despite her sophisticated appearance. “Dad's been working such long hours lately, and Mom... well, she always says we need to let Alan find his own path.”

“Why don't you ask Alan if something's wrong?” Angie suggested gently. “Ask if there's anything you can help with?”

“Maybe.” Alice attempted a smile that didn't reach her eyes. “Sorry to bother you with my worries. Thanks for listening to me. It’s a lovely evening here on the yacht. I'd better go find my parents.”

Angie watched Alice walk away, her senses pinging with a warning. Something about the conversation felt important - not just the words but Alice's carefully controlled concern. The young woman moved through the crowd like someone carrying a heavy secret.

Ellie appeared beside her, the lights catching her necklace. “Learn anything new from Alice Benson?”

“Just that she and her brother aren't as close as they used to be, but there's something more there – like there’s something she's afraid to say.”

“That's interesting.”

Their conversation was interrupted by a sudden scream that cut through the music and chatter. The sound came from the stern, followed by Alan Benson's voice, tight with panic.

"Someone has fallen overboard!"

Josh, Chief Martin, and several crew members rushed to the stern. The band stopped playing mid-song. Worried murmurs replaced the festive atmosphere as guests crowded toward the railings to see what happened.

Courtney hurried over to her sisters, slightly breathless. "Rufus and I heard heated words between two men about ten minutes ago, by the rear deck. We couldn't see them, and we couldn't make out what they were saying, but it was definitely an argument."

Mr. Finch approached, his usual gentle expression replaced by grave concern. "It's Roman Alderwood who has gone overboard. He's an art dealer from Boston who has a summer home here. He had been talking to Alan Benson earlier."

"Is he all right?" Angie asked, though something in Mr. Finch's face suggested the worst. Behind them, Betty was already on her phone, presumably calling emergency services.

"I don't know. The water's deep near the stern. Someone said he might have hit his head."

The minutes seemed to stretch endlessly. Josh

coordinated with the crew while Chief Martin took charge of the increasingly agitated crowd. Rose Harrington had grown pale, and Lincoln guided her to sit down, his arm protective around her shoulders.

Finally, Tom and Jenna joined their group, both looking shaken. Tom's tuxedo was wet - he must have helped with the rescue attempt.

"They pulled the victim from the water," Tom reported quietly. "He's dead."

A chill seemed to settle over the evening air around the yacht. As emergency vehicles' lights began flashing on the dock, their sirens eerily silent, Angie caught sight of Alan Benson slipping away from the crowd, his phone pressed to his ear. His face was ashen, and his hands were shaking.

Nearby, his sister watched him go, her expression filled with worry. Dr. Benson and his wife stood frozen near the dessert table, their faces white from shock.

As Chief Martin began quietly interviewing guests, Alan Benson was still on his phone, now speaking urgently in tones too low to hear.

"This isn't a coincidence," Mr. Finch murmured to Angie. "Roman Alderwood's gallery specialized in authenticating valuable artwork. He was particularly known for his expertise in Dutch masters."

The man's statement hung in the air like the music that had so abruptly ceased. Around them, the beautiful evening had transformed into something ominous, the twinkling lights now seeming more like warning beacons than decorations.

The harbor waters lapped quietly against the yacht's hull, as if trying to whisper something that would soon come to light. What had started as a glamorous charity event had just become something dark and worrisome.

And somehow, Angie was sure, this death would connect to their investigation in ways they had yet to discover.

19

The family room seemed almost surreal at midnight with everyone still in their formal wear. The young women's gowns glittered in the lamplight while the men loosened their bow ties. Chief Martin sat heavily in an armchair, his tuxedo slightly rumpled, exhaustion evident in his face. The room felt both elegant and unsettled, like the evening itself.

Angie served coffee from a silver pot while Ellie distributed slices of vanilla bean cake with raspberry filling. The familiar comfort of sharing food felt especially important tonight. The cats joined the others - Euclid on Courtney's lap and Circe with Mr. Finch - both seeming to sense the serious mood of the gathering.

"Alan Benson claims he was speaking with

Roman Alderwood about fifteen minutes before the incident," the chief began, gratefully accepting his coffee. "According to Alan, he could smell alcohol on the man's breath. He suggested Roman might have been drunk, using drugs, or suffered some kind of medical emergency. He told me Roman seemed agitated and confused during their conversation."

The coffee cups clinked softly against their saucers in the quiet room. Outside, a gentle rain had begun to fall, its patter against the windows adding to the late-night atmosphere.

"Did other guests report the same thing?" Jenna asked, absently smoothing her gown. Her bracelet sparkled, creating tiny dancing reflections on the walls.

"One other person mentioned that Roman seemed preoccupied and short-tempered," the chief replied, "but no one else noticed anything particularly wrong with him. He was in his late sixties, so a medical emergency is certainly possible. We'll have to wait for the autopsy and toxicology reports, though that could take a while."

"Did Alan Benson know Roman Alderwood?" Josh questioned, standing near the fireplace. He'd removed his tuxedo jacket but still looked every inch the successful businessman.

The chief nodded, setting down his coffee cup. "Slightly. His parents knew him socially - not friends exactly, more like acquaintances. They moved in the same circles and attended many of the same events. Roman was an art dealer, and both Alan and Alice have shown interest in art."

Courtney stroked Euclid's fur thoughtfully. The cat's purring provided a soothing counterpoint to the tension in the room. "Rufus and I heard heated words coming from the stern a few minutes before Mr. Alderwood fell over the railing."

Rufus, his English accent more pronounced with fatigue, nodded in agreement. "We heard the voices but couldn't see who was speaking. I was about to investigate, but the argument stopped abruptly. We didn't hear anything more after that."

"Could it have been Alan Benson arguing with Mr. Alderwood?" Mr. Finch asked softly, while Circe watched the chief intently from her spot on Mr. Finch's lap. The cat's eyes seemed to gleam with understanding.

"It's possible." The chief sighed, looking even more tired. "We'll keep interviewing the attendees. Some people had already left when we started taking statements."

"It was such a nice evening until this happened."

Rufus said what they were all thinking. His hand found Courtney's, and he squeezed it. He looked at the chief. "Do you think it was foul play?"

The chief was quiet for a moment, considering his words carefully. "I'm leaning that way," he admitted finally, "but only because Mr. Alderwood was an art dealer and because of the art heist at the Harringtons. The timing feels significant. Hopefully, I'm wrong and it was just a terrible accident." He rubbed his eyes wearily. "I'll keep you posted."

"Did Alan tell you what he and Mr. Alderwood were talking about?" Jenna asked the chief.

"Art. That was all Alan said."

"Would you like more coffee?" Angie offered, but the chief shook his head.

"Thanks, but I should get home. Lucille's waiting up, and tomorrow will be a long day of interviews and paperwork."

They rose to say their goodnights, the rustle of silk gowns mixing with the continuing patter of rain against the windows. Courtney walked the chief to the door while the others began clearing coffee cups and plates with subdued movements.

The clock in the hall struck one, its chime seeming especially solemn. Another mystery had landed in their laps, and somehow, they all knew it would connect to the stolen paintings. How many more lives would be affected before they uncovered the truth? Outside, the rain continued to fall on Sweet Cove, as if trying to wash away the evening's tragic events.

But some things, they knew, couldn't be so easily cleared away.

Sleep refused to come despite Angie's exhaustion. The events of the evening kept replaying in her mind like a film she couldn't stop - the argument no one quite heard, Alan Benson's distant behavior, and Roman Alderwood's fatal fall. She tossed and turned beside Josh's sleeping form, her thoughts cycling through the suspects they had.

Alan Benson kept returning to her list. Alan's secretive behavior and new mysterious friends, along with Alice's worried observations about her brother, made him a suspect. Then there was their father's nervous manner whenever the art theft was mentioned. She'd dismiss them, then something she thought of would bring them back onto the list of suspects.

There were the Collins gallery owners - Beth's

fear, Nathan's absence, their connection to the art world, and the strange phone call to Mrs. Harrington that originated near their gallery.

Donald Prior popped into her mind next. He'd been a volunteer at the holiday house tour, gave a false address on his application, and was seen at the Brimfield outdoor market before disappearing moments later.

Finally giving up on sleep, Angie slipped from bed, careful not to wake Josh. The Victorian was quiet at this hour, moonlight creating strange shadows in the rooms as she made her way to their apartment's kitchen. Maybe some warm milk would help settle her mind.

She had just reached for the pan when soft footsteps made her turn. Gigi stood in the doorway, rubbing her eyes, her favorite stuffed dog clutched in one arm.

"Honey, why are you up?" Angie asked softly, moving to kneel beside her daughter.

"I had a dream." Gigi's voice was small in the moonlit kitchen. "That bad man was in it."

A shiver ran down Angie's spine, raising goosebumps on her arms. "What bad man?"

"The one from the stores in the field." Gigi yawned, but her eyes were focused on something beyond the kitchen. "I think he's outside."

Angie followed her daughter's gaze to where Euclid sat on the windowsill, his orange fur silvered by moonlight. The cat's posture was rigid, and his attention was fixed on something in the yard below. As they watched the cat, his tail began to twitch - not the lazy swish of contentment, but the sharp, agitated movement that signaled trouble.

Moving carefully to avoid creaking floorboards, Angie approached the window. The Victorian's grounds were shadowy, the garden beds and pathways transformed by darkness into unfamiliar shapes. At first, she saw nothing unusual, but then...

Euclid let out a low, threatening hiss, his fur bristling.

"What was the man doing in your dream?" Angie asked Gigi, trying to keep her voice calm while her heart raced.

"He was looking at some papers," Gigi mumbled, clutching her toy tighter. "In my dream, he was angry about the papers."

Another hiss from Euclid made Angie's decision. "Let's get you back to bed, sweetheart. Then Mommy needs to talk to Daddy."

After tucking Gigi in with extra kisses and making sure her night light was on, Angie hurried back to her bedroom. Josh was still sleeping soundly with one arm thrown across her empty pillow.

"Josh," she whispered, shaking his shoulder gently. "Josh, wake up."

He came awake instantly, years of marriage to Angie having taught him that middle-of-the-night wake-ups usually meant trouble. "What's wrong?"

"There's someone in the yard. Gigi had a dream about him - the man from Brimfield. Euclid's acting strange."

Josh was already pulling on jeans over his pajama bottoms. "I'll get Rufus."

While Josh went down the hall to wake their brother-in-law, Angie returned to the kitchen window. Euclid hadn't moved, his eyes still fixed on something she couldn't quite see in the shadows of the old maple tree. In a moment, Circe joined him on the windowsill, her eyes seemingly locked onto something in the yard.

The sound of quiet footsteps told her Josh and Rufus were back. Both men were dressed hastily, but they moved with purpose.

"Where exactly?" Rufus's eyes were bright and focused.

"Near the maple tree," Angie whispered.

"Euclid's been staring at that spot for the last ten minutes."

Josh checked that his phone was fully charged. "I'll go around to the front of the house while Rufus takes the back. Stay inside and lock everything. If we aren't back in fifteen minutes, wake Ellie and Jack. Then call Chief Martin."

"Okay. Be careful, you two," Angie urged, her heart pounding as the men slipped out of the apartment, down the staircase to the foyer, and into the darkness.

She moved from window to window, trying to track their progress. The garden, so lovely during the day, had become a maze of threatening shadows. Euclid followed her, his low growl a constant warning.

Suddenly, a figure darted from behind the maple tree - a man in dark clothing, moving with surprising speed. Josh and Rufus spotted him simultaneously, their shouts breaking the night's silence.

"Hey! Stop!"

The figure sprinted toward Beach Street with Josh and Rufus in pursuit. Angie watched, helpless, as they disappeared around the corner, their footsteps fading into the distance.

Minutes that felt like hours passed before she

heard them returning, their pace slower now, defeated. When they came back inside, both men were breathing hard.

“We lost him,” Josh reported grimly. “He took a shortcut through the neighbor’s yard and disappeared.”

“He got a head start on us or we would have caught him, but we got a decent look at him,” Rufus added, running a hand through his disheveled hair. “Young man, tall, athletic build. He was wearing dark clothes and a baseball cap pulled low.”

“Did he look like Donald Prior?” Angie asked, remembering Gigi's words about 'the man from the stores in the field.'

“It could be.” Josh nodded. “Though it was too dark to be certain.”

Euclid had finally relaxed his vigil, moving to weave between their legs as if checking that everyone was safe. From down the hall came the sound of Gigi's door opening.

“Mommy?” her small voice called. “Is the bad man gone?”

Angie hurried to scoop up her daughter. “Yes, honey. Daddy and Uncle Rufus scared him away. Everything's safe now.”

But as she held Gigi close, exchanging worried

looks with Josh and Rufus over her head, Angie knew that safety was becoming increasingly relative. Someone had been watching their house – and Angie was sure it was someone connected to their investigation.

"I'll call the chief," Josh said quietly, reaching for his phone.

Outside, the night had grown still again, but it was a stillness that felt more threatening than peaceful. Somewhere in Sweet Cove, a man was running through the darkness, carrying secrets that seemed increasingly dangerous.

And Gigi's dream about papers made Angie wonder - what were those documents?

The answer, she suspected, would lead them closer to understanding not just the art theft, but perhaps Roman Alderwood's death as well.

20

It was late when Angie finished her end-of-day routine at the bakery. She wiped down the display cases, now empty of the day's treats, and double-checked the prep list for tomorrow's baking. The familiar scents of vanilla and cinnamon still lingering in the air didn't help ease her growing concern about the investigation.

Recent events kept replaying in her mind - Roman Alderwood's death, the mysterious figure in their garden, and Alan Benson's distant behavior reported by his sister. Each piece seemed important, but the complete picture remained frustratingly unclear.

She had just stepped into the main house, planning to change before dinner, when her phone rang.

Beth Collins's name on the screen surprised her - the gallery owner had been distinctly unhelpful during their previous visit.

"Ms. Roseland? This is Beth Collins." The gallery owner's voice sounded strained, almost desperate, nothing like her usual controlled tone. "Could you come to the gallery?"

"I can come, yes. What day would you like to meet?"

"Today. Right now." The words came out sharp, urgent, and with an underlying tremor that set off Angie's intuition.

"Oh. Okay," Angie said, caught off guard by the demand. "Is anything wrong?"

"No," Beth snapped, then immediately disconnected the call.

Angie stared at her phone, startled by the abrupt ending. Something in Beth's tone set off warning bells - not just urgency, but fear.

Quickly, she texted Courtney:

> Can you come with me to the Collins Gallery? Beth just called - something's wrong.

The response came instantly.

Yes. Pick me up outside the candy shop. Give me five minutes.

Moving quickly, Angie changed from her flour-dusted bakery clothes into fresh jeans and a sweater. The spring afternoon was cooling rapidly, and the drive to Brimfield would take at least fifty minutes. As she headed downstairs, she ran into Jenna.

"I just finished up working in the studio for the day. Everything okay?" her twin asked, immediately sensing her sister's tension.

"I'm not sure. Beth Collins just called, sounding strange. Courtney and I are going to check it out."

"Do you need me to come too?"

"Better not – it might spook her, but if you don't hear from us in two hours..."

"I'll call the chief," Jenna finished. "Be careful."

The drive through Sweet Cove was peaceful, with tourists strolling through the town.

Courtney was waiting outside the candy shop. She slipped into the passenger seat with a worried expression. "What's going on? Has something happened with Beth?"

"All I know is that she asked me to come right now, and then she hung up. Her voice sounded off. Almost scared."

"Weird." Courtney watched the familiar scenery give way to countryside. "Did you tell Chief Martin?"

"I didn't have time."

"I'll text him." Courtney pulled out her phone. "He needs to know where we're going."

Angie made a face. "In case we don't come back?"

"Yup." Courtney looked at her sister. "Is this a good idea to go without the chief?"

"If we go with the chief, Beth might clam up. I think it's worth it for just the two of us to go, and anyway, she has no reason to harm us. We don't know anything."

"You're right." Courtney nodded. "I'm just being paranoid. Though after everything that's happened, it's justified."

They drove in silence for a while. The sky was awash with shades of pink, blue, and gold from the setting sun, but the beauty felt somehow dangerous today.

After nearly an hour, the converted mill building appeared ahead, its red brick glowing in the late light. The river provided its constant background music as they pulled into the parking lot. Only one other car was there - Beth's silver Mercedes.

Inside, the gallery felt different – darker and

more oppressive than during their previous visits. The valuable artwork on the walls seemed to watch them as they entered. Beth emerged from the back rooms almost immediately, and both sisters were struck by her appearance. Her usual polished look had vanished - her face was pale with dark circles under her eyes suggesting sleepless nights. Her clothes hung loosely, as if she'd lost weight rapidly.

"Thanks for coming," she said, her voice tight. "I want to show you something."

They followed her through the gallery into the store room at the back of the place, their footsteps echoing in the empty space. The air felt stuffy as they entered the windowless room. Beth led them to a storage closet, reached inside with trembling hands, and removed something wrapped in torn brown paper. She placed it carefully on a nearby table.

"I found this at the back of the closet." She pulled away a piece of the paper, revealing what lay beneath. "Is this one of the paintings you're looking for?"

Courtney gasped. "Oh, my gosh." She and Angie stared at the unmistakable artwork before them - the distinctive style and the historical significance immediately apparent.

"It's a Dürer?" Angie asked, though she already knew the answer. The masterpiece seemed to glow even in the dim storage room light.

"Yes. Does this belong to the Harringtons? Is it one of their stolen paintings?" Beth's lips were pressed in a tight line, her hands still shaking as they hovered near the frame.

"I'm not sure," Angie said carefully, though her heart was racing. "I'll take a photo with my phone and send it to Chief Martin to confirm." She snapped several pictures, trying to keep her hands steady while documenting every angle.

Courtney examined the piece without touching it.

Beth waved her hand around. "I hadn't seen it in the closet before. I tore the brown paper it was wrapped in, and well, here it is." Her voice cracked slightly on the last words.

"Where did it come from? Did your husband purchase it from someone?"

"He must have, but he didn't tell me about it." Beth ran her hand over her face, suddenly swaying slightly. The strong, confident gallery owner they'd first met seemed to have crumbled away, leaving someone fragile and frightened in her place.

"Come on, sit down." Courtney quickly guided her to a chair.

Angie's phone rang - the chief returning her message. After a brief conversation, she turned to Beth. "The chief is coming out here. He'll be here in about forty minutes."

Beth barely responded, just lifting her hand before letting it drop limply into her lap.

"The painting is one of the ones stolen from the Harringtons," Angie confirmed quietly. "Chief Martin confirmed it."

"Could there be others in the storage room?" Courtney questioned, already moving toward the closet.

Beth's voice was barely above a whisper. "I checked. That was the only one wrapped in brown paper."

"I'm going to look anyway." Courtney disappeared into the closet.

Angie pulled a chair closer to Beth. "Where's Nathan?"

Beth's eyes flashed with sudden anger. "I don't know. I haven't seen him." She took a shuddering breath and tears formed in her eyes.

"Nathan must have purchased this painting," Angie said carefully.

"He must have." Beth's tone was harsh, her hands balling into fists. "Receiving stolen goods... I'd like to kill him. We're breaking up. I'm filing for divorce."

The words hung in the air, heavy with emotion.

"Has he ever done this before?"

"Not to my knowledge." Beth wiped roughly at her eyes, smearing her expensive mascara. "But now I wonder what else I've missed; what other lies he's told me."

Courtney emerged from the closet. "I didn't find anything else."

"I'll be right back." Angie walked out to the front room, her investigative instincts taking over. At the transaction desk, she examined receipts and notes pinned to the small board on the wall. A yellow sticky note caught her eye – 'Douglas P.' written in hasty handwriting. The name meant nothing to her, but she filed it away mentally. A quick check of the desk drawers revealed credit card slips and gallery paperwork, but nothing obviously suspicious.

By the time Chief Martin arrived with two officers, the sun had completely set. The gallery's track lighting created dramatic shadows as the chief interviewed Beth while his officers conducted a search of the premises. Beth seemed to have retreated into herself, answering questions in a monotone, her earlier emotion locked away behind a wall of shock.

The drive home was quiet at first, both sisters processing what had happened. The headlights cut through the gathering darkness as they wound their way back to Sweet Cove.

Finally, Courtney spoke. "The Harringtons will be so happy to have at least one painting back."

"If only we could find the others," Angie said, "but this is definitely progress."

"What do you make of Beth and Nathan's situation?"

"I think there's more to it than she's saying. The timing of their separation, finding the painting..." Angie shook her head. "And where is Nathan? How did he get the Dürer?"

Courtney added, "Everything seems to be connecting somehow - Nathan Collins, Donald Prior, maybe Alan Benson, and Roman Alderwood's death... we're just missing the thread that ties it all together."

The Victorian's lights were welcoming as they pulled into the driveway. Through the windows, they could see their family gathered in the living room - Jenna pacing while she talked on the phone, Ellie sipping tea, and Mr. Finch sitting with his ever-present sketchbook.

"It's one step forward," Courtney said as they walked to the house, "but something tells me we're not going to like where this leads."

Angie nodded, remembering Beth's contained fury and her obvious fear. One painting recovered, but so many questions remained. Where was Nathan Collins? What connection did he have to the theft? And most importantly - where were the other paintings?

The mystery was slowly unraveling, but each answer seemed to bring new questions. Still, they had made progress - one masterpiece would soon be returned to its rightful owners. It was, as Courtney had said, one step forward.

As they walked into the warmth of their home, both sisters knew that until all their questions were answered, their work wasn't done. The weight of the evening's discoveries followed them inside, where their family waited to hear what new turns their investigation had taken. Outside, the spring night settled over Sweet Cove, holding secrets close.

21

It was late afternoon on Robin's Point as the Roseland sisters, Mr. Finch, the two cats, and Gigi and Libby gathered. After the other night's frightening encounter with the stalker, they felt drawn to this special place where their connection to their grandmother had always been strongest. Seabirds wheeled overhead, their calls mixing with the constant rhythm of waves against the cliffs below.

The Point held decades of family history. Their grandmother's cottage had once stood near the cliff's edge, a cozy haven where the sisters had spent countless summer days. Though the cottage was long gone - lost in a complicated land dispute years ago - the space still held their memories.

Many years after the residents of the Point lost

their houses and before Angie and Josh had met, Josh and his brother purchased the land from the town and had the beautiful Sweet Cove Resort built on it. When Josh fell in love with Angie, he bought out his brother's ownership share in the resort and had a lawyer draw up papers that returned most of Robin's Point to the Roseland sisters.

None of them had built on it, and they didn't think they ever would. The Roselands had made sure the Point was always open to the public so people could stroll the grounds, picnic under the trees, and admire the stunning views of the ocean.

Josh's purchase and return of the land to the sisters had felt like the closing of a circle, a wrong finally made right.

Now families spread blankets on the grass where their grandmother's herb garden had once flourished. Children played tag where the sisters had sat under a large Maple tree where their grandmother had read them stories. The Roselands maintained their grandmother's belief that natural beauty should be shared.

"It's perfect weather for this," Angie said, watching Gigi and Libby skip ahead, their energy seemingly boundless. Euclid and Circe followed at a more dignified pace, with their tails held high as they supervised their young girls.

The sisters carried several beach chairs while Mr. Finch brought a picnic basket filled with drinks and snacks. The evening breeze carried the smell of the sea, along with the subtle scent of beach roses that still grew wild along the cliff's edge.

They found a perfect spot on the grassy overlook where their grandmother used to sit and watch the sunset. Several other groups were scattered across the Point - young couples walking hand in hand, families playing Frisbee, and elderly residents enjoying the view from benches Josh had installed along the paths.

"Remember when all this was private cottages?" Courtney asked as they set up their chairs. "Now look at how many people can enjoy it."

"Josh did a wonderful thing returning the land to the four of you," Mr. Finch agreed, settling into his chair with a contented sigh.

"It always feels peaceful here." Courtney smiled, watching boats bob gently on the waves below. The evening light shined over the water, while sailboats headed back to harbor for the night.

Ellie nodded, touching her necklace. "I can feel Nana all around us, especially on evenings like this."

"Being on the Point always helps clear my mind," Angie added, slipping on her sunglasses. After the other night's frightening encounter with the stalker, she especially needed this peaceful moment. Even now, she couldn't shake the image of that shadowy figure beneath their maple tree.

"I remember when Nana would set up her easel right about here," Jenna said, closing her eyes as if seeing the past. "She'd paint for hours while we played nearby. Oh, and remember how she taught us to identify healing plants?"

"And how we'd help her dry herbs in the cottage kitchen," Courtney added. "Though we probably caused more chaos than help."

"I imagine your nana loved having you with her in the summers," Mr. Finch suggested, his voice warm with affection for his adopted family.

Courtney chuckled. "Most of the time. We were kind of balls of energy. She must have been exhausted by the end of summer."

"We kept her young." Ellie grinned, the breeze playing with her hair.

"Remember when Jenna tried to cook breakfast for all of us one morning?" Courtney asked. "The kitchen looked like a category 4 hurricane had come through." She turned to her sister. "Jenna?"

But Jenna wasn't listening. Her eyes had taken on a distant look, fixed on something only she could see. The other sisters recognized that expression immediately - it was the same look their grandmother had worn at times.

"What's wrong?" Angie asked, moving closer to her twin. The temperature seemed to drop slightly, though the air was still warm.

Jenna remained silent, still staring into the distance. Even the girls stopped playing, sensing something important was happening. After what felt like an eternity, she whispered, "I can see her."

Angie leaned closer, her protective instincts kicking in. "Who? Who can you see?"

"Nana."

Courtney jumped up. "You see Nana? Where?"

"Shhhh," Ellie cautioned. "Don't break the moment."

They watched in respectful silence as Jenna remained transfixed. Even the cats seemed to sense the importance of the moment, sitting perfectly still nearby, their eyes focused on the same spot Jenna watched. The only sounds were the waves below and the distant laughter of children playing.

Finally, Jenna blinked and swayed slightly. Angie grabbed her arm, helping her sister back into her chair while Mr. Finch quickly offered water from his backpack. The color had drained from Jenna's face, but her eyes were bright with emotion.

Libby skipped over, her face glowing with excitement. "Did you see Nana? I saw her by the cliff. She waved at me!"

Jenna gathered her daughter close, her hands trembling slightly. "Yes, honey, I did see her. Did Nana say anything to you?"

"No, she just waved, but she was smiling, like she used to in the photos."

"Did she speak to you?" Angie asked her twin, noting how pale Jenna had become. The air around them felt charged, like just before a summer storm.

"No, but she showed me something." Jenna's voice was barely above a whisper. "Her face... it kept changing. It turned into a man's face, and then to another man's face, but the second man was facing away from me so I couldn't see him." She rubbed her temples, clearly drained from the ghostly vision.

"What about the first man?" Angie pressed gently, while Courtney poured more water and Ellie moved closer to offer support.

"He looked familiar, but it was foggy and I couldn't make out the features. Then Nana turned back into herself. She smiled and nodded at me. It made me feel happy to see her, but also... worried somehow."

"Maybe the men's faces will become clearer later," Ellie suggested. The necklace at her throat seemed to gleam more brightly than usual.

"I saw them too, Mommy," Libby announced matter-of-factly, still nestled in Jenna's arms.

Everyone stared at the little girl, surprised by her calm certainty. Even Mr. Finch leaned forward in his chair, his expression intent.

"What did you see, sweetheart?" Courtney asked gently.

"The men Nana was showing us. They were like shadows at first, but then they got clearer."

"Did you ever see them before?" Angie questioned her niece, while Gigi moved closer to listen.

"I saw the first face before. It's that bad man who was standing by the tree at night."

"How do you know?" Angie asked carefully. "You were asleep when he was near the tree. You weren't in the room with me, Libby."

"I know. I saw him in my dream. It's the same man we saw at the outside market. The place with all the booths."

The adults exchanged looks. Donald Prior. The pieces were starting to come together.

The girls returned to their play, but the atmosphere had shifted. The ghostly visit had confirmed their suspicions while raising new questions about the second, unknown man. Even the endless ocean view seemed somehow different, as if shadows lurked beneath its sparkling surface.

"I think she's right," Jenna said weakly. "The face did resemble Donald Prior. Maybe the other man's identity will come to me later."

"Donald Prior and the second man must be working together," Courtney concluded.

"My head is swimming," Jenna admitted. "Can we take a break from talk of suspects?" She took a deep breath of ocean air. "I'd really like some ice cream."

"That's the best thing you've come up with all day." Courtney smiled, already starting to pack up.

They loaded the chairs and supplies back into the van and then made the short drive to Coveside. The harbor area was already busy with evening visitors who walked along the brick sidewalks that led past restaurants, cafes, and small shops, while boats bobbed at their moorings in the harbor.

The transformation of Coveside from working waterfront to tourist destination had taken decades, but now hanging flower baskets decorated the antique lampposts, and the old fish processing buildings had become galleries and boutiques, but somehow it had retained its authentic charm, especially in the evening when tourists and locals mixed easily on the busy sidewalks.

"I'm suddenly feeling really energized," Jenna said as they walked, her color returning. The vision seemed to have lifted a weight from her shoulders, though questions still lingered in her eyes.

"I wish I could see Nana again," Ellie said quietly, watching a family of tourists taking photos by the harbor.

"It's okay, Ellie. Nana can still see you," Courtney assured her. "We're all different and have unique skills. Jenna can see ghosts, and you have other abilities."

"You're the one who's most like Mom," Jenna reminded her. "We all know you're going to be as powerful as she was."

Ellie's eyes widened as she touched her necklace. "I hope I can be half as skilled as Mom."

The ice cream shop was doing brisk business, but soon they were all settled on benches near the harbor, enjoying their treats as the sun set. Boats returned to their slips, their running lights beginning to twinkle in the gathering dusk.

The peaceful moment was broken when Angie suddenly stiffened, her ice cream forgotten. Her vision spun wildly, making her feel nauseated. As quickly as it came, the sensation passed, but she found herself standing up and turning in a slow circle, scanning the crowd of evening visitors.

"What is it, Miss Angie?" Mr. Finch asked, concern evident in his voice.

"I... I thought I could feel Donald Prior nearby." She shook her head, still searching the faces around them. "I don't see him though."

"That doesn't mean he wasn't here," Mr. Finch pointed out. "He may have gotten lost in the crowd."

"We need to make sure we lock the house up tight every night and arm the alarm," Ellie said firmly. "And maybe Orla can come over and put a protection spell around the Victorian."

"Well, look at you," Courtney said with a smile, "advocating for casting spells. I never would have believed it. You've come a long way from fearing our abilities to willingly accepting them, sis."

"People change," Ellie replied, trying to suppress her own smile. "Sometimes they have to."

As the sky darkened and the harbor lights began to twinkle, they made their way back to the van. Courtney held Mr. Finch's arm while Angie pushed the stroller with the girls singing and the cats trilling. Jenna and Ellie walked arm-in-arm behind them.

The evening had brought them closer to understanding the mystery but had also reminded them of what was most important - their family connections, their shared heritage, and the special gifts passed down through generations.

As they drove home to the Victorian, the lights of Sweet Cove spreading out around them, Angie felt their grandmother's appearance had been more than just a comforting visit. She had come to warn them to prepare them for what was coming. Were they ready for whatever that might be?

The moon rose over the ocean, its light silvering the waves and casting long shadows across Robin's Point. Somewhere in those shadows, Donald Prior was hiding. But tonight, at least, the Roselands had been reminded they weren't facing this challenge alone.

Their grandmother's spirit watched over them, just as she always had.

22

Sweet Cove's Main Street had transformed into a wonderland of color and activity for the annual May Festival Stroll. Antique street lamps, their black iron recently polished, wore festive ribbons in spring colors. In front of the shops, flower boxes and ceramic pots overflowed with tulips, pansies, and early roses, their colors echoing the bright awnings over the shop windows.

The brick sidewalks, worn almost smooth by generations of feet, were crowded with tourists and locals alike. Children clutched balloons while their parents browsed sidewalk sale tables. The sound of a local band playing near the town green mixed with the laughter and conversation, while delicious aromas floated on the air from restaurants and food trucks parked at strategic intervals.

Mr. Finch had transformed the front of his and Courtney's art gallery into an impromptu studio. He sat at an easel, demonstrating sketching techniques while two young employees helped visitors create their own artwork. His eyes twinkled as he guided a young girl's hand, showing her how to capture the shape of a flower.

Next door at the candy shop, Courtney and Rufus presided over a candy display that drew constant crowds. Glass jars of colorful sweets caught the sunlight while Rufus used his charm to convince customers to try their newest fudge flavors.

"I'm a fudge expert," Rufus told the customers. "That's partly because my last name is actually Fudge."

Many of the customers didn't believe him until he took out his driver's license and showed them his name.

Jenna's jewelry booth showcased her latest designs, and the crystal suncatchers she hung up created rainbows that danced across her display. Her handcrafted pieces seemed to capture the fun of the festival, and she'd already sold several of her ocean-inspired necklaces to happy tourists.

Right next to her twin sister, Angie's pastry booth filled the air with the scent of fresh-baked goods and rich coffee. She'd been baking for hours since she'd been up all night anyway, and her hard work showed in the perfectly arranged displays of scones, muffins, and her famous lemon bars. A line had formed the moment she opened.

"Your coffee cake is amazing," a customer told her, already halfway through a slice. "We're here from Boston, and nothing there compares to this."

Angie was thanking her when she spotted Chief Martin making his way through the crowd. Despite the festive atmosphere, his expression was serious as he approached her booth.

"Quite a turnout," he said, accepting the coffee she automatically poured him. "Though I'm actually here about the visitor you had the other night."

Angie glanced around to make sure no customers were within earshot. "It was definitely the same man Gigi saw at Brimfield," she said quietly. "She dreamed about him before she even saw him in the yard."

The chief leaned against the booth's counter, appearing casual though his eyes constantly scanned the crowd. "Tell me again exactly what happened."

"I couldn't sleep," Angie explained, automatically rearranging her display as she talked. "Gigi came out of her room, saying she'd dreamed about 'the bad man from the stores in the field.' Then she said she thought he was outside."

"And he was."

"Yes. Euclid spotted him first - you know how the cats sense things. The man was standing under the maple tree in the sideyard. Josh and Rufus chased him, but he got away through the neighbor's yard."

The chief made a note in his small notebook. "Tall, athletic build, dark clothes, baseball cap?"

"That's what Josh and Rufus said. He only got away because he heard them coming."

A group of tourists approached the booth, and Angie paused to serve them. The chief watched her as she worked, his mind clearly processing the information she'd shared with him.

Through the crowd, they could see Courtney demonstrating how to make saltwater taffy, her audience captivated by the process.

"There's something else," Angie said when the customers moved on. "Gigi mentioned he was looking at papers in her dream and that he was angry about them."

The chief's expression sharpened. "Papers? What kind of papers?"

"She didn't know, but..." Angie lowered her voice as another festival-goer passed by. "Given everything that's happened, could it be documentation for the paintings? Provenance papers? Forgeries, maybe?"

"Could be," the chief agreed. "The Harringtons would have detailed records for their collection, insurance documents, and authentication certificates. Maybe this guy was creating false documents."

Their conversation was interrupted by a burst of applause from the art gallery, where Mr. Finch had just completed a detailed sketch of the town harbor. He smiled and handed it to a delighted young woman as Courtney called out from her booth, "He's quite the artist, isn't he?"

The chief watched the scene thoughtfully. "I've posted extra patrols in your neighborhood," he said finally, "and we're looking into any short-term rentals in the area. If this man's been watching your house, he must be staying somewhere nearby."

"The timing seems important," Angie mused, handing a blueberry muffin to a waiting customer. "First the heist, Roman Alderwood's death, and now this..."

"My thoughts exactly. Alderwood was known for

authenticating artwork. If there was something questionable about one of the stolen paintings..."

The festive sounds of the May Stroll continued around them - children laughing, the band starting another tune, and Rufus's voice carrying as he described their chocolate varieties to customers. Beneath it all, Angie felt a current of tension, like storm clouds gathering on a sunny day.

"I should make my rounds," the chief said, finishing his coffee. "Keep your eyes open. A desperate person might take bigger risks."

As he moved away through the crowd, Angie caught Jenna's eye at the next booth. Her twin's expression told her she'd overheard enough to be concerned. They'd have to tell the others about the chief's warning.

The May Festival Stroll would continue all day, but for the Roseland family, every shadow might hide a watcher, and every stranger might be a threat. The simple pleasure of the spring festival had been complicated by the knowledge that somewhere in Sweet Cove, a desperate man was searching for something - and he seemed to think the Roselands knew something about it.

Angie turned to serve another customer, maintaining her smile while her mind worked on the puzzle. Papers that made someone angry enough to risk being caught, a dead art authenticator, and stolen masterpieces.

The pieces were there, but the picture they formed was still unclear.

And somewhere in the festival crowd, could their mysterious watcher be watching them even now? A shudder ran over Angie's skin at the thought.

The lunchtime crowd had swelled along Main Street as Angie made her way toward the sandwich shop. She had a long list of orders from her family and their employees, all of whom were too busy with the festival to break away themselves. The spring sunshine warmed the brick sidewalks, and music from a street performer's guitar floated on the breeze.

She nearly bumped into Alan and Alice Benson coming out of the bookstore. The twins looked more relaxed than they had at the yacht party, dressed casually for the festival. Alice wore a flowered sundress while Alan had exchanged his usual preppy look for jeans and a Red Sox t-shirt.

"It's a beautiful day," Alice said brightly, her

smile genuine. "Alan and I decided to hang out together today." She glanced at her brother with obvious happiness, as if wanting Angie to notice they'd worked through whatever tension had existed between them.

"Perfect weather for the festival," Angie agreed. She couldn't help noticing how the twins seemed relaxed and happy together. "Though I imagine everyone's talking about what happened on the yacht."

The twins shared glances, their demeanor shifting slightly.

"It was awful," Alice said softly. "I still can't believe it happened."

Alan moved from foot to foot, looking uncomfortable. "The police interviewed me again this morning about my conversation with Mr. Alderwood."

A group of tourists passed by, their chatter about local restaurants momentarily drowning out the conversation. When they'd moved on, Angie reached for her phone.

"Actually, while I have you both here..." She pulled up the photo of Donald Prior. "I'd like you to look at something. Do you know this person?"

Alice leaned in first, her brow furrowed in concentration. "I don't recognize him. Should I?"

But Alan's reaction was immediate and unmistakable. He stepped closer to the phone, his casual manner completely vanishing. "I know him by his stance - that particular way he holds himself. He was at school with me, but he dropped out junior year. He was studying art history."

"His name is Donald Prior?" Angie asked carefully, watching both twins' reactions.

"No, that's not his name." Alan shook his head. "It's Douglas Palmer. He's from Woodstock, Connecticut." He paused, and then added, "He wanted to be an art dealer. He got an internship at some gallery in Boston."

Angie's heart skipped a beat at this good fortune. "Do you recall the name of the gallery?" She tried to keep her voice neutral-sounding despite her racing heart.

Around them, the festival continued with children running past with painted faces and the smell of kettle corn drifting from a nearby vendor.

Alan thought for a moment, then shook his head. "I don't remember, sorry. It was somewhere in the Back Bay area, I think."

"Have you been in touch with him?" Angie questioned, noticing how Alice watched her brother intently during this exchange.

"No, not for a year," Alan told her. "I haven't seen him since he dropped out of school."

"What did you think of him?"

"We weren't best friends or anything." Alan shrugged, his casual manner returning. "He could be fun, but he wasn't really into studying or doing well in school. He was always looking for a get-rich-quick scheme."

Alice touched her brother's arm lightly. "You never mentioned him before."

"There wasn't much to mention," Alan replied.

The festival crowds surged around them, creating a strange bubble of privacy in the midst of the celebration. A balloon vendor passed by, his colorful wares bobbing in the spring breeze, creating an oddly festive backdrop to the serious conversation.

"Well, thank you very much for the information," Angie said, already planning to share this revelation with her family. "It's very helpful."

"Of course." Alan nodded, clearly ready to end the conversation. "We should let you get those sandwiches. Everyone must be hungry by now."

As the twins turned to leave, Alice hesitated.

"Angie?" Her voice was soft, uncertain. "Is Douglas Palmer ... is he involved in something?"

"Chief Martin just needs to talk to him," Angie assured her, though she noticed Alan had stiffened at his sister's question.

"Come on, Alice," Alan said. "We promised to meet Mom and Dad for lunch."

Angie watched them disappear into the festival crowd, noting how Alan steered his sister away with a hand on her elbow.

Pulling out her phone, she immediately dialed Chief Martin's number. The call went to voicemail after several rings.

"Chief, it's Angie. I just ran into the Benson twins. Alan identified our mystery man – he says his real name is Douglas Palmer from Woodstock, Connecticut. They were in school together. Call me when you can."

The festive atmosphere of the May Stroll suddenly felt like a thin veneer over something darker. Douglas Palmer, not Donald Prior, was a dropout art history student with a taste for get-rich-quick schemes.

The sandwich shop was just ahead, its line stretching out the door. As Angie took her place in line, she went over the conversation with the Benson twins and couldn't believe the stroke of good luck. Thanks to Alan, they finally knew the young man's real name.

It felt like a breakthrough but also like opening a door to something potentially dangerous.

The May Festival Stroll continued, bright and merry, but Angie's mind was already racing ahead to what this new information might mean - and what their next move should be.

23

When she returned to her booth, Angie told Jenna what she'd learned from the Benson siblings.

"His real name is Douglas Palmer?" Jenna asked. "You saw the name Douglas P on a sticky note on the desk at the Collins's art gallery."

"Nathan, and maybe Beth, must be in on the art theft. Douglas Palmer must have sold the stolen paintings to them," Angie guessed. "I called Chief Martin, but he didn't answer. I left a message for him asking him to call me."

After more speculation, the sisters returned to running their booths.

Thirty minutes later, Angie's vision struck. She had been working at her booth with Louisa, her friend and employee, arranging fresh-baked scones on display plates, when the familiar disorienting sensation washed over her. The festive sounds of the street fair faded away, replaced by terrifying images that made her grab the table for support.

"Angie?" Louisa's concerned voice seemed to come from very far away. "Are you all right?"

But Angie couldn't respond. In her mind's eye, she saw the Collins gallery, its elegant rooms dark and shadowy. Beth Collins was there, her face contorted with fear as a figure advanced toward her. The scene was frustratingly foggy, the attacker's identity hidden in shadow, but Beth's terror was unmistakable.

When the vision finally released her, Angie found herself sitting in a chair Louisa must have brought over, her hands shaking as she fumbled for her phone.

"Jenna," she called to her twin at the next booth. "I need you."

Jenna hurried over, immediately recognizing her sister's post-vision state. "What did you see?"

"Beth Collins," Angie managed, her voice trembling. "She's in danger. Someone's going to attack her at the gallery." She was already dialing Beth's number, but the call went straight to voicemail. "Beth, it's Angie Roseland. You're in danger. Please get somewhere safe and stay there. Call me back immediately."

Angie looked at her twin. "I have to go to the Collins's gallery."

"I'll text Ellie," Jenna said, pulling out her phone. "You shouldn't go alone. I'll stay here and handle the two booths."

Minutes later, Ellie drove to Main Street and helped Angie into her van. "I'm going with you," Ellie insisted, sliding into the driver's seat. Her necklace seemed to pulse slightly in the sunlight.

The drive to Brimfield felt endless, though Ellie pushed the speed limit the entire way. When they pulled into the gallery parking lot, both sisters felt an immediate sense of wrongness. The building's windows were dark despite the 'OPEN' sign still displayed.

"Something's not right," Angie whispered as they approached the door.

It swung open at their touch.

The gallery's usual elegant atmosphere had been replaced by heavy silence. Their footsteps echoed on the hardwood floor as they moved inside. Then they saw her - Beth Collins lying motionless on the floor, a dark stain spreading beneath her.

Both sisters gasped. Ellie rushed forward, her

hands shaking as she searched for a pulse while Angie pulled out her phone to call Chief Martin.

Before she could make the call, footsteps sounded from the back of the gallery. Roland Stone, the Harringtons' son-in-law, emerged from the shadows, followed by Douglas Palmer. The pieces suddenly clicked into place with horrifying clarity.

"Well, well, if it isn't Douglas Palmer, the art thief and murderer," Ellie said with disgust, still kneeling beside Beth's body. Her voice was steady despite the fear Angie could see in her eyes.

"Roland is the murderer, not me," Palmer protested, his face pale.

Roland brushed past his accomplice with a snarl. "Keep your mouth shut," he muttered. He looked at Angie. "Give me that phone."

Angie placed her phone on the floor and kicked it toward him, her mind racing for options. "Where's Nathan?" she asked.

Roland's glare was cold. "Nathan can't be reached right now. Get in the backroom."

"You stole those paintings from your in-laws," Angie said, trying to buy time. "Why did you do it?"

Roland's eyes widened as he pulled a gun from his belt. "That's none of your business. If you hadn't made it your business, you wouldn't be about to die."

Something shifted in the air then. Ellie rose slowly to her feet, her presence suddenly filling the room. "If you weren't a thief and a killer, you wouldn't be about to go to prison." The ends of her long blonde hair began to lift, floating as if in an invisible breeze.

Angie felt her sister's power building and looked around desperately for something to use as a weapon.

"What's up with your hair?" Douglas asked, his voice shaking as he took a step back.

"Don't move, either of you," Ellie commanded, stepping forward with her arms outstretched. The air seemed to crackle around her.

"Stupid witch." Roland aimed the gun at Ellie.

What happened next seemed to unfold in slow motion. Ellie's eyes grew wide, fixed on the gun. Light flickered from her fingertips as energy gathered around her. A guttural sound like nothing Angie had ever heard emerged from her sister's throat, and suddenly the gun began to twist and bend as if it were made of rubber.

Roland screamed and dropped the deformed

weapon. Angie seized her chance, grabbing a letter opener from the desk and holding it threateningly.

Douglas turned to flee, but Ellie used her telekinetic power to flip a chair into his path. He sprawled hard on the floor, and Angie quickly bound his hands behind his back with her belt.

"What's going on? Who are you? Get me out of here! Get away from me!" Douglas wailed, thrashing uselessly.

Roland stood frozen for a moment, his face chalk-white. Then he shook himself and bolted for the backroom.

He managed only three steps before Ellie thrust her palms toward him. Bolts of electricity arced across the space, striking him squarely in the back. He swayed, then crashed face-first to the floor, unconscious.

"I didn't know you could do that," Angie said, staring at her sister in amazement.

Ellie shrugged, though she looked slightly dazed. "Neither did I."

Angie hugged her sister tightly. "Well, I'm very glad you did," she whispered, then went to find a sheet in the backroom. She carried it back to the gallery, and together with her sister, they covered Beth's body with a gentle reverence.

"If only we'd gotten here sooner..." Ellie sighed.

Angie nodded sadly, brushing tears from her eyes. She reached for her phone, but before she could make the call, she noticed movement outside. "The police are here."

Chief Martin burst in with two officers, their weapons drawn. Relief flooded his face when he saw the sisters. "Thank heavens you're okay."

Douglas was still struggling against his bonds. "Get me out of here! Those two are witches!"

The chief gestured for an officer to secure Douglas. "Who's on the floor over there?"

"Roland Stone, the Harringtons' son-in-law," Angie explained. "We're pretty sure he stole the paintings with Douglas's help. He killed Beth Collins. We don't know where Nathan is."

A look of concern washed over the chief's face as he walked over to the window to call for an ambulance.

When he returned to them, the sisters quietly explained what had happened. "Mr. Finch called me," the chief told them. "He'd just gotten home from the festival to pick something up, and he found Euclid and Circe going crazy – howling, screeching, and racing through the house. Mr. Finch knew you were in danger and told me where you'd gone. I used the siren the whole way here."

"Ellie saved us," Angie said proudly. "We'll tell you the details later, but my sister really surprised me today."

"I surprised myself," Ellie admitted, touching her necklace.

"All I can say is thank heavens you did." The chief hugged them both, his usual professional demeanor softened by relief.

As emergency vehicles began arriving outside, their lights painting the gallery walls in alternating red and blue, Angie looked at her sister with new understanding. Ellie had fully embraced her powers, and in doing so, she had saved their lives.

"Mom would have been so proud of you."

Ellie's eyes misted over.

The mystery of who stole the Harringtons' paintings was solved but at a terrible cost. Beth Collins had paid with her life for her husband's involvement with Roland and Douglas.

The Harringtons would have to deal with the devastating knowledge that their son-in-law had betrayed them so completely, and there were still questions that needed answering, but those were concerns for tomorrow.

Tonight, they were simply grateful to be alive, thankful for their special gifts, and so appreciative for the family bonds that had once again helped them survive danger.

Outside, the evening settled over the converted mill building, the river's constant rush a reminder that life would go on. Inside, amidst the aftermath of violence, two sisters stood together, their powers and their love for each other stronger than ever.

24

The Victorian's backyard was transformed for the family cookout, with Ellie's gardens providing a spectacular backdrop. Climbing roses cascaded over the white pergola in shades of pink and red, while beds of irises, peonies, and early lilies created waves of color throughout the yard. The long outdoor dining table beneath the pergola gleamed with blue and white linens, and mason jars filled with fresh-cut flowers marked each place setting.

Euclid and Circe supervised the preparations from their favorite garden bench; occasionally getting up to inspect the setup. When Josh and Tom brought out platters of raw burgers for the grill, both cats perked up, their attention focused on the possibility of dropped morsels.

"Don't even think about it," Angie warned them as she arranged bowls of potato salad and coleslaw on the buffet table. "You've already had your dinner."

Circe merely blinked at her, while Euclid made a strategic move closer to the grill where Tom was checking the temperature.

Gigi and Libby darted through the yard, testing each game station Josh and Rufus had set up - corn-hole boards painted with beach scenes, croquet wickets arranged across the level grass, and a ring toss that seemed designed to tangle small feet.

"Careful near the flower beds," Ellie called out, arranging cushions on the outdoor furniture. Her gardens were her pride and joy, and today they seemed to glow, as if sensing the celebration to come.

"Everything looks perfect," Mr. Finch declared, emerging from the house with Betty. They carried platters of Angie's freshly baked pies - apple, cherry, and blueberry - their crusts still slightly warm from the oven, and a butterscotch and pecan bread pudding. The cats immediately abandoned their grill surveillance to investigate the new possibilities.

"Shoo, you two." Betty laughed, skillfully maneu-vering past them to arrange the pies on a separate table. "Though I can't blame them - these pies smell heavenly."

As the afternoon sun began its slow descent, guests arrived steadily. Chief Martin and his wife Lucille brought their famous coleslaw, while Orla and Mel Abel appeared with an enormous pot of baked beans. The Harringtons came bearing bottles of wine, their faces showing both the joy of having their paintings returned and the lingering sadness of Roland's betrayal.

"The house feels whole again," Rose said quietly to Angie as they arranged wine glasses. "Though I still can't quite believe everything that happened. You know, we never liked Roland. He was always in a bad mood."

Chief Martin drew the sisters aside as they added more chairs near the fire pit. Euclid and Circe followed, settling nearby as if interested in the conversation.

"I thought you'd want to know about Alan Benson," he said, keeping his voice low. "Turns out he's been investigating the theft on his own all this time. That's why he seemed so distant to the family lately."

"Really?" Angie watched across the yard where Alan was teaching Gigi and Libby how to play croquet, his sister Alice laughing at their attempts. The twins looked more relaxed than they had in weeks.

"He was upset that something like this could happen in his neighborhood," the chief explained, absently scratching Euclid behind the ears. "That's why he'd been distant with Alice - he was completely consumed with trying to solve the crime. Actually, he had some good insights, though he should have come to us sooner."

"At least that mystery's solved," Ellie said, watching Circe stalk through her flower beds on patrol. "Though the bigger revelations were far worse than we imagined."

The full story had emerged over the past few days. After meeting Douglas at a lecture in Boston, Roland masterminded the entire heist and recruited the young man to help him. The truth about Roman Alderwood's death was particularly chilling. After the heist, Roland had approached Alderwood at his office in Boston to ask about the stolen paintings' worth. When Alderwood grew suspicious of his questions, Roland was worried the man might contact the authorities to report the odd discussion they'd had. When he found out Alderwood would be at the charity event, Roland decided to slip him a lethal dose of opioids to get rid of him, once they were on the yacht.

"The drowning wasn't even the cause of death," the chief added, accepting a glass of lemonade from Mr. Finch, who'd joined their group. "The toxicology report showed enough opioids to be fatal on their own."

"And Nathan Collins?" Courtney asked, coming up behind them.

"The police found his body in his home office in Brimfield. Nathan received the stolen paintings and was going to help ship them to buyers overseas, but the men had a falling out. Roland had to eliminate him as a loose end, but Nathan had hidden the remaining paintings in the trunk of his car." The chief shook his head. "Each one carefully wrapped in brown paper, just like the Dürer that Beth found."

"Do you think Beth knew?" Jenna wondered, watching the children play tag around the garden beds.

"We'll never know for sure," the chief replied. "But given her final actions, trying to return the painting..." He left the sentence unfinished.

"I don't think she was part of it," Angie told them. "I don't believe she knew what was going on until she found the Dürer in the closet of the gallery."

As the sun began to set, Tom and Josh lit the tiki torches that lined the garden paths. The flames created dancing shadows among the flowers while the fire pit crackled to life, sending sparks up into the darkening sky. The children chased fireflies across the lawn, their laughter mixing with the sounds of cricket song and distant waves.

Even the cats seemed to feel the evening's magic. Euclid had claimed a prime observation spot on the stone wall bordering Ellie's herb garden, while Circe wound elegantly between guests' legs, accepting treats and attention with regal grace.

Lara looked different as she walked around, chatting with the other guests; gone was her usual perfectly coordinated designer outfit, replaced by casual jeans and a soft sweater. Her hair fell in natural waves, and her face looked younger without its usual mask of careful makeup.

She found Angie and Ellie by the dessert table, declining wine in favor of sparkling water. "Ever since I went through my medical training, I've been trying to be perfect," she confessed, watching her sister, Brenda, teaching a group of children how to make daisy chains. "I've been trying to create a perfect life, but in doing so, I lost something important."

"What was that?" Ellie asked gently.

"The ability to just... live. To enjoy simple moments." Lara's smile held a touch of sadness. "I lost sight of what really matters - love, trust, relaxing, and being with family and friends. Look at Brenda - she's got it all figured out without even trying.

"Brenda and I have been spending a lot of time together," Lara continued, her expression softening. "Making art in her studio, having coffee, just talking. It feels good, really good. That's what I want to focus on for the rest of my life. Maybe someday soon, I can find the part of me that I lost and get in touch with it again ... find the me that I used to be."

"It seems like you're well on your way," Angie told her warmly, watching as Circe approached Lara and rubbed against her legs - a sign of approval the cat rarely bestowed on visitors.

Brenda came over and slipped her arm through Lana's. "I need to steal my sister away. I want to play ring toss with her."

Lara smiled. "I'd love to."

The two women walked across the lawn with their arms around each other's waists.

The evening progressed with a nice easy rhythm.

Josh and Tom kept the grill going with burgers, chicken, and vegetables, while the buffet table remained laden with salads, sides, and desserts. Along with the pies, the chocolate cake and the strawberry-lemon bread were both big hits. Children's voices mixed with adult laughter, along with the soft background music Rufus had chosen.

“Who's up for the cornhole tournament?” Courtney called out, organizing teams as twilight deepened. Even Chief Martin and Lucille joined in, partnering with Mr. Finch and Betty to everyone's surprise.

“I'll have you know I was cornhole champion at the police picnic three years running,” the chief announced, landing a perfect shot through the hole.

“Show off,” his wife, Lucille, called fondly from her seat near the fire pit.

The tournament grew increasingly competitive, with good-natured heckling and cheering from the sidelines. Euclid and Circe watched from the stone wall, heads swiveling to follow the bean bags' trajectories as if judging the technique.

“Did you see that?” Gigi exclaimed as her father scored another point. “My Daddy's the best!”

“I think my dad is good too,” Libby said loyally, which had the nearby adults hiding smiles.

As darkness settled fully over the garden, the tiki torches and strings of fairy lights created a magical atmosphere. The fire pit drew people like moths, its warm glow perfect for quiet conversations and marshmallow toasting.

"Who wants s'mores?" Courtney called, producing bags of chocolate and graham crackers. A line of children quickly formed, with more than a few adults joining in.

"Remember when Nana used to make these for us at her cottage?" Ellie asked her sisters, perfectly toasting a marshmallow to golden brown.

"She always said the secret was patience," Jenna smiled, watching her daughter attempt to toast three marshmallows at once.

The cats had settled near the fire, their fur gleaming in its light. Even they seemed to sense the special nature of the evening, maintaining their best behavior despite the tempting array of food still available.

As the night deepened and younger children began to fade, guests started departing with hugs and promises to gather again soon. Finally, only the family remained, settled comfortably around the fire pit with coffee and the last slices of pie.

"I have to say," Mr. Finch mused, accepting a

fresh cup of coffee from Betty, "this has been one of our more interesting cases."

"Interesting isn't quite the word I'd use," Courtney said, curled against Rufus on a double chair. "Terrifying at times."

"But we solved it together," Angie pointed out. "And everyone's safe now."

"Thanks to Ellie's newfound powers," Jenna added, making her sister blush.

"I still can't believe I did that," Ellie admitted, touching her mother's necklace. "It was like something just... opened up inside me."

"Your mother would be so proud," Mr. Finch said softly. "All of you make her proud every day."

The fire crackled and popped, sending sparks up to join the stars. Night-blooming jasmine added its sweet scent to the air, mixing with the lingering aroma of grilled food and wood smoke. Gigi and Libby had fallen asleep on a nest of blankets, their faces still showing traces of chocolate from eating s'mores.

Euclid and Circe had migrated over to the sleeping children, assuming their usual protective positions. Their quiet purring added to the peaceful atmosphere of the gathering.

"It seems like summer is going to be good this year," Josh said, his arm around Angie.

"Peaceful, I hope," Tom added with a grin.

"Oh, I don't know about that." Courtney laughed. "We do have a talent for finding trouble."

"Or maybe trouble finds us," Jenna suggested.

"Either way," Mr. Finch said, raising his coffee cup, "here's to family, to safety, and to whatever mysteries come next."

They all raised their cups in agreement, while the two fine felines trilled and swished their tails. As the fire burned lower and the night deepened, none of them felt inclined to move inside. The Victorian stood proud behind them, its windows glowing with warm light. Like their family, it had weathered storms and had come through stronger. Now it watched over their gathering like a beloved guardian, a reminder of all the adventures they'd shared and all those yet to come.

The ocean breeze carried the promise of warm days ahead, of beach picnics and evening walks, and of simple pleasures shared with the people they loved most in the world.

THANK YOU FOR READING! RECIPES BELOW!

Books by J.A. WHITING can be found here:
amazon.com/author/jawhiting

To hear about new books and book sales, please sign up for my mailing list at:
jawhiting.com

Your email will never be sold, shared, or spammed.

If you enjoyed the book, please consider leaving a review. A few words are all that's needed. It would be very much appreciated.

BOOKS BY J. A. WHITING

SWEET COVE PARANORMAL COZY MYSTERIES

SPELLBOUND BOOKSHOP PARANORMAL COZY MYSTERIES

LIN COFFIN PARANORMAL COZY MYSTERIES

CLAIRE ROLLINS PARANORMAL COZY MYSTERIES

MURDER POSSE PARANORMAL COZY MYSTERIES

PAXTON PARK PARANORMAL COZY MYSTERIES

ELLA DANIELS WITCH COZY MYSTERIES

SEEING COLORS PARANORMAL COZY MYSTERIES

OLIVIA MILLER MYSTERIES (not cozy)

SWEET ROMANCES by JENA WINTER

COZY BOX SETS

BOOKS BY J.A. WHITING & NELL MCCARTHY

HOPE HERRING PARANORMAL COZY MYSTERIES

TIPPERARY CARRIAGE COMPANY COZY MYSTERIES

BOOKS BY J.A. WHITING & ARIEL SLICK

GOOD HARBOR WITCHES PARANORMAL COZY MYSTERIES

BOOKS BY J.A. WHITING & AMANDA DIAMOND

PEACHTREE POINT COZY MYSTERIES

DIGGING UP SECRETS PARANORMAL COZY MYSTERIES

BOOKS BY J.A. WHITING & MAY STENMARK

MAGICAL SLEUTH PARANORMAL WOMEN'S FICTION COZY MYSTERIES

HALF MOON PARANORMAL MYSTERIES

VISIT US

jawhiting.com

bookbub.com/authors/j-a-whiting

amazon.com/author/jawhiting

facebook.com/jawhitingauthor

bingebooks.com/author/ja-whiting

SOME RECIPES FROM THE SWEET COVE SERIES

Recipes

STRAWBERRY-LEMON BREAD

INGREDIENTS

2 cups unbleached all-purpose flour

¼ teaspoon salt

1 teaspoon baking soda

½ cup chopped walnuts (optional)

2 large eggs

½ cup sugar

8 Tablespoons unsalted butter, melted and cooled

¼ cup milk

1 Tablespoon grated lemon zest

2 cups fresh strawberries, cut into ½ inch pieces

INGREDIENTS for GLAZE:

¼ cup fresh lemon juice

3 Tablespoons sugar

DIRECTIONS

Heat oven to 350°F.

Lightly butter an 8½ x 4½ x 2½ inch loaf pan.

DIRECTIONS FOR BREAD:

In a large mixing bowl, sift together flour, baking soda, and salt.

Add the walnuts and stir to combine.

In another bowl, lightly beat the eggs with the sugar; then mix in melted butter, milk, lemon zest, and strawberries.

Make a well in the middle of the dry ingredients, and add the liquid mixture to it.

Stir with a wooden spoon just until the dry ingredients are moistened. Do not overmix. The batter will be fairly thick.

Pour the batter into the prepared loaf pan.

On the middle rack, bake until the bread is lightly browned or until a toothpick inserted in the center comes out clean, about an hour and 5 minutes.

Cool in the pan on a rack for 15 minutes.

DIRECTIONS FOR GLAZE:

Place lemon juice and sugar in a small saucepan and stir to dissolve the sugar.

Place over medium heat and simmer until the mixture is syrupy and reduced by half (about 4-5 minutes). Don't let it burn.

Remove the pan from the heat.

Remove the bread from the pan.

Pour the warm lemon glaze over the top of the loaf.

Cool completely before serving.

MIX-IN-THE-PAN CHOCOLATE CAKE

INGREDIENTS

6 squares (6 ounces) bittersweet or semisweet chocolate, or 1 cup of semisweet chocolate chips

1 cup heavy cream

⅔ cup packed light brown sugar

2 large eggs

1⅓ cups self-rising cake flour

DIRECTIONS

Heat oven to 350°F.

Using an 8- or 9-inch square baking pan (no need to grease it), put chocolate and ¼ cup of cream in the pan.

Place pan in oven for 3-5 minutes.

When the cream just begins to bubble, remove

the pan from the oven and whisk until cream and chocolate have blended. If the chocolate isn't fully melted, return the pan to the oven for 1-2 minutes and then whisk again.

Whisk in remaining cream.

Add sugar and whisk to blend. Then whisk in the eggs until smooth – remember to stir into the corners of the pan.

Add the flour. Stir with a rubber spatula until well blended – scrape the sides and bottom of the pan to be sure to blend everything.

Bake 30 to 35 minutes until a toothpick inserted in the center comes out clean.

Cool the cake in the pan on a wire rack.

Cut into 9 squares.

BUTTERSCOTCH PECAN BREAD PUDDING

INGREDIENTS

3 Tablespoons unsalted butter, room temperature

¾ cup lightly packed dark brown sugar

2 cups milk

1 teaspoon baking soda

Pinch of salt

2 eggs

1 teaspoon vanilla

4 cups stale bread cubes with crusts removed

½ cup pecan halves (optional)

DIRECTIONS

Set the oven at 350°F.

Butter an 8-inch square baking pan.

In a medium saucepan, melt the butter over low heat, then add the brown sugar and cook until the sugar melts and turns syrupy.

Gradually stir the milk into the sugar mixture; then stir in the baking soda and salt. Allow the mixture to cool completely.

In a mixing bowl, whisk together the eggs and vanilla. Stir a little of the milk mixture into the eggs, then add the remaining egg mixture to the saucepan and blend well.

Arrange the bread cubes in the baking pan and sprinkle the pecans over them.

Pour in the egg mixture and transfer the baking dish to the oven.

Bake the pudding for 40 to 50 minutes or until it sets and the top is browned.

Remove from oven and serve with vanilla ice cream.

Enjoy!

Made in United States
North Haven, CT
28 February 2025